THE VALIANT
VIRGINIANS

THE VALIANT VIRGINIANS

JAMES WARNER BELLAH

FOREWARD BY FLETCHER PRATT

MAPS BY RAFAEL PALACIOS

CUTTING EDGE

ISBN-13: 978-1-954840-48-5

A shorter version of this novel, under the title *Tales of the Valorous Virginians,* appeared serially in *The Saturday Evening Post*

Published by
Cutting Edge Books
PO Box 8212
Calabasas, CA 91372
www.cuttingedgebooks.com

For
Brigadier General Henry Barlow
Cheadle, U.S.A., Rtd.,

who was the first regimental commander to be made a general officer in World War II—on the field of battle, by presidential order. A professional who loved his 16th Infantry—a regular regiment with fifty-four battle honors dating to 1798, to which the General added the taking of Oran, in the finest tradition of the First Infantry Division.

FOREWORD BY
FLETCHER PRATT

THIS IS A BOOK about very young men in war, becoming veterans while their officers are learning how to handle them. Tactically, that is; from the very beginning the leading figure in the book knew a good deal about the personal side of handling men, both here and on the factual record. It is also, in accordance with modern taste and Mr. Bellah's own particular skill, a book about the minor incidents that involve the rear-rank private, and that are often of a great deal more importance to him than how the battle came out. This is regardless of the fact that he went into the battle out of a certain idealism and in the future is going to be deeply affected by its major results—if he has any future after the battle.

So far as my memory goes, this technique has not often been applied to the Civil War, and most especially to the Virginia end of it. Put the combination Civil War-Virginia into the hopper and you will usually come out with a beautiful girl in crinoline on a plantation and a couple of dashing young captains who say "Suh," have a high sense of honor, and clank their spurs. The rear-rank private is on hand in such stories purely as a spear-carrier. This time he is the center of the picture, and it must be a good deal nearer what the war was really like. The average Virginia soldier was not really a plantation product.

Moreover, Mr. Bellah has heightened his effect by a thoroughly honorable use of dialect. Not the kind that confuses the issue and makes things difficult to understand, but that which gives an acceptable reproduction of the speech rhythms and thought patterns of the people doing the talking. This whole series of "takes" is told in a kind of easy drawl, as though they came from the mouth of someone who was at least a close participant in the events described.

The nature of those events is also worthy of some attention. You cannot have a war or a war story without battles, especially when, as in the present case, the framework requires that each tale be wrapped around some major occasion of the war. The usual trouble is that the battle becomes so much the center of the picture that the author feels obliged to make it his leading character and ends up writing history instead of fiction. The hero has to carry the message that saves the day. Mr. Bellah has neatly avoided this trap. The major events take place all right, but he is quite aware that battles, for all their intensity of action and emotion, make up a very small part of war, either counting the amount of time spent on them or the amount of thought devoted to them—except afterward, when old soldiers get 'round to telling lies. Most of the time is spent in worrying about things like the soup tureen or the silk dress—which you will find chronicled hereinafter.

Jeb Stuart pops into and out of a couple of the stories, looking pretty much to the life, but the major historical character is Stonewall Jackson. It is hard to give a true picture of a general from a soldier's point of view; you can only say how he looked to the soldiers, and in this case the portrait is probably just about accurate, except that Jackson's sternness seems a little written down, and so is his religious side. But perhaps the private didn't know about these things, or didn't think them remarkable. There seem to have been a fair number of praying colonels in the C.S.A.

And in any case this is Jackson before the war took on its subsequent intensity, while it still seemed possible that the issue could be decided in the terms and with the proportionate casualties of the other wars America had engaged in up to that time.

It should not be forgotten that when the Civil War opened we were military amateurs and pretty naive ones at that. One of the special excellences of this book is the manner in which it shows Davin Ancrum and Roan Catlett turning from skylarking boys into the veterans who fought that titanic series of struggles on the long road to Appomattox.

As this book closes, those struggles have just begun with the Seven Days' Battles, and even these take place offstage. The area covered is the first year of the war, and except toward the end, there is not much that can be said to background these stories. Mr. Bellah's valiant Virginians saw it all, and knew as much as anyone else about what was going on. The skirmishing around Harper's Ferry in the early days of the conflict, with which the book opens, was exactly that—a series of confused clashes in which not many people got hurt or accomplished very much. Bull Run, where the fighting was hot enough and angry enough for a time, was a clash between two groups of men only playing at soldier so far. The Union army marched out to where it knew it could find the Confederates and they had a battle. That was all. At Ball's Bluff, McClellan had ordered a reconnaissance in force across the Potomac, and then withdrew its supports, with results cited in these pages.

It is only when we come to Kernstown that strategy begins to raise its head. Jackson took a beating there and it was a solid one, but he was probably right in claiming that this was one of those battles where it did not matter so much who had won the formal victory as that there had been a battle. The Shenandoah Valley was the back door to Washington, and if the Confederates were going to be active there, Washington would have to see that it was strengthened, no matter how much the result might weaken the forces supposed to be conducting an offensive against Richmond along the peninsula between the York and the James.

The phrase "supposed to be" is used advisedly. The background of the last two stories is the discovery by the Confederate generals—Lee deserves most of the credit—that McClellan, who was around Richmond on two sides, close enough to hear the churchbells ring, and with considerably superior forces, was not going to take any aggressive action until he had still more men. Very well, they would take action against him.

Jackson attacked the Union force at the north end of the Shenandoah, defeated it and sent it flying. Lincoln and Secretary Stanton—there was no one below them who had the authority to move the troops of more than one army—ordered one army eastward into the Valley from West Virginia, reinforced the beaten troops already there, and recalled a whole corps that was marching to join McClellan, sending it westward into the Valley in a triple pincers movement on Jackson. This was when Stonewall's men earned the name of "foot cavalry." By hard fighting and incredible marching he hit each jaw of the pincers in turn, damaged it badly, and was down before Richmond attacking McClellan's right wing, before the Federals knew what had happened.

It is observable that more backgrounding is necessary as the war goes on and things get complicated. These stories are concerned with the change that made the complications.

THE VALIANT VIRGINIANS

When you cross the Blue Ridge and come into the Shenandoah Valley, the breed of man changes subtly. He grows taller against the western mountain bastions of Virginia and his voice shades soft in primal courtesy, nor does he speak as often, for a great many of the things men talk of elsewhere were resolved forever long before he was born—and brook no further discussion. His memories of race are deep within him, his habits of life patterned by them. There is right and there is wrong still left for his decision, but the dividing line between is more sharply drawn across God's canvas of the mountains than it is in the cities of the world.

Of this breed was Roan Catlett, born six miles from Deerfield, where the women the Catletts married "kept the blood and kept the progression." A few miles north his cousin Forney Manigault, second boy of old Judge Manigault, first drew milk from his mother's lady breasts and knew the whispering winds in the towering oaks of Manigault. Lastly there was Davin Ancrum, cousin to Forney but not to Roan, but a boy grown tall to walk with men.

There were Indian mounds they played among and because of Yorktown and New Orleans and Bladensburg so close still upon their boyhood, they were the Indians who defeated Braddock. A downed and shattered redcoat was the capstone of the growing American tradition, so they destroyed a British Army once more in the savage play of youth—Roanoke Colony being gone so far into the mists of history by their time that the Indian once more had attained to a nobility they would emulate.

They broke their own horses and coerced the blood of Timoleon and Bright Eyes to the flat saddle. Their fathers taught them to shoot. The old men of Chapultepec and Cerro Gordo taught them their history—that there is a time of peace and a time of war and that the inalienable right to bear arms is a part of the dignity of free men.

Their mothers gentled them with native courtesy so that they might develop a deference for age, the obligation of protection for youth more helpless than their own, and a sense of decency toward women so that some day they might look a girl in the eye full and take her hand for better or for worse—but whatever, forever.

But long before Forever started, the shore batteries of Charleston Harbor fired on Sumter and the young United States locked its fledgling muscles into an inter-family struggle that no one won and no one lost—for Appomattox marked the birth of soul and stature of this land of ours, and the legend of the gallant Army of Northern Virginia is still the deep, firm beat of its stout heart.

Roan Catlett, Forney Manigault, Davin Ancrum. Remember their names for in their time they were men. And being men, the essence of immortality came upon them. As their grandfathers did not die at Brooklyn Heights, so their sons did not die at San Juan or El Caney, their grandsons at Chateau Thierry or in the Argonne Forest, their great-grandsons with RCT 116 on Omaha Easy Red—or in the skies above Heartbreak Ridge in far Korea.

For this is a century of war, and like it or not, wars must be won by us when we are born to them. That what happens to one now has happened to one's blood long ago, is sometimes a comfort in time of present trial. So let us go back and watch the preparation a country underwent in order that it might be strong and unified, fit to meet the trial of leadership that the years would bring.

Long, long after Appomattox if you had asked Roan or Forney or Davin if they had fought, their eyes would have come up slowly *and level and they would have said, "I was out with Stonewall Jackson."*

But in that spring of 1861, Forney trudged up the road to the Catlett place and he said "Roan—you goin'?" Roan looked at him with the Catlett eyes that were like stiff fingers pronged upon him.

"Yes."

Forney traced dust with his boot toe. "What about Davin— he's only fifteen. The Senator won't let him go unless you promise to look out for him."

"I'll promise. Well, Forney? Come on."

So the hill-billy muleteers and the gentry squadrons of Turner Ashby were formed and the great cavalry tradition of J. E. B. Stuart galloped through the land. May the echo of their hoofbeats never die in the memories of U.S. 56197111 and his present companions in arms; for it is a comforting thing in age to have been out with Jackson, but a greater thing by far to know that one stands rifle in hand faced toward the savage doctrine that man may live only in duress under the heel of his more opportunist fellow—whereas his innate dignity is a fact before God that seven centuries of thought and prayer and bloodshed have brought to fullest flower in this broad and pleasant land.

"Well, Forney? Come on."

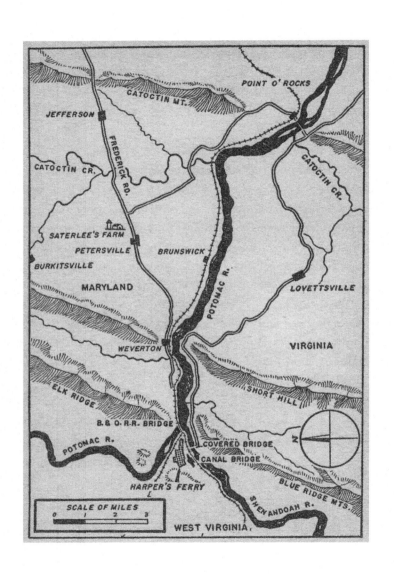

FIRST BLOOD AT
HARPER'S FERRY

ROAN CATLETT NEVER ATE hog after the Cross Keys fight.
He'd vomit if he smelled it cooking. They got loose in the
woods after Cross Keys and ate the Yankee dead. But that first
spring of the war, when the Valley companies marched up the
Shenandoah to take the arsenal at Harper's Ferry, Roan was still
a powerful hog-eating man.

Cap'n Murt Patton marched the Short Mountain Company.
He was in Mexico last war with Winfield Scott. Vera Cruz,
Molino del Rey, Cerro Gordo and Chapultepec. Sharp fighting,
to hear the Cap tell of it over a jug, and he had plenty of time
to tell of it, for he was too old and too fat to ride a horse any
more, so he led the company up, riding in Doctor Breckenridge's
brougham.

By the time the company got as far north as Harrisonburg,
the Cap was having everybody call him major. The folks in New
Market gave him such a send-off two weeks later that he promoted himself up to colonel. By the end of the month, when the
company tore itself loose from Winchester, he put a bunch of
feathers in his old Army hat, divided the boys up into two regiments of ten men each and rode his carriage into Harper's Ferry,
general of the brigade.

At Harper's Ferry it was like Market Day every day. There
wasn't any nonsense about drilling or shooting at the mark, and
there were so many other self-promoted militia generals arguing
who commanded over what, that they let the soldiers be. Besides,

everybody owned his own horse and his own gun and nobody was used to being told what to do, except by his own pappy—and most of the Short Mountain boys had 'listed themselves up for the war to get quit of that. All but Davin Ancrum. Davin wasn't yet sixteen. Senator Ancrum only let Davin go along if he gave his promise to do what Roan Catlett told him. That was the way it was agreed, otherwise Davin couldn't get to go.

All told, at Harper's Ferry there were about forty-five hundred boys gathered to fight by the time Virginia was taken into the Confederacy on May seventh. Folks said this Abe Lincoln, fifty miles southeast in Washington, had about a hundred and fifty thousand Yankee soldiers, while forty-five miles north, in Chambersburg, Pennsylvania, a Yankee general named Patterson had about twelve thousand more. Right smart odds.

Roan Catlett turned seventeen that spring, but he was berry brown already with the Valley sun, and his hair was dark red-black, like a new colt's, so he looked about twenty. He was four inches over six feet and he could clamp his teeth into the off rim of a hogshead, tilt it to him and lift it, full to the heading with tobacco, clear off the ground. That way he always had betting money in pocket.

Roan got sparking a pert snip of a girl over west of town in the part they call Bolivar, and one night the girl let drop that her uncle was the biggest breeder of Chester Whites in Western Maryland. The name was Satterlee and this hog farm lay about twelve miles over the Potomac. Now, a Chester White is white, with pink skin like a baby's. As the breeders say, it possesses good carcass qualities, which means it eats well when roasted. And finally—to Roan's thinking—they originated the breed in Chester, Pennsylvania, which made them sure-enough Yankee hogs and free as the summer breeze for the taking.

You couldn't sleep at night anyway, on account of the trains rumbling through. The Baltimore and Ohio Rail Road runs double track through Harper's Ferry from Point o' Rocks twelve miles down toward Washington, to about sixteen miles west of Martinsburg. There was talk of blowing out the covered bridge to get quit of the noise, but the railroad was working for us as well as for the Yankees. So the bridge stayed in and nobody got much sleep.

Roan got Davin to ride up to Satterlee's farm with him the night after he found out about it, and reconnoiter those Chester Whites. Now, Roan and Davin weren't kin. Roan was Forney Manigault's cousin. So was Davin. But they weren't cousins to each other. Forney was slow-thinking. He had to chew things out in his mind for the right of them. So Roan didn't tell Forney about this hog expedition.

About the fifth roast-hog breakfast in a row that the company was enjoying, Forney Manigault looked over across at Roan. "Roan," he said, "where y' takin' Davin nights?" Forney is Judge Dabney Manigault's second boy. The judge rode circuit forty years in the county and never took court oath. Said his word was his bond and he wasn't going to fancy it up with oaths like the liars did. There was the judge's look in Forney when he spoke to Roan.

"I'm takin' him ridin'," Roan said, and he turned slow and let his eyes finger Forney's eyes. Roan had the Catlett eye. So pale blue it looked like it ought to hurt. Only man in the world you could feel his eyes on you like stiff fingers. Only man, that is, except Stonewall Jackson.

"Davin ain't grown yet," Forney went on. "He needs his sleep. He's my cousin. You leave him be nights. Y'hear?"

"He may be yore cousin," Roan said, "but his daddy told him to mind me. And that's who he's goin' to mind until we get the orders countermanded."

Making him out to be a boy to be looked after like that before everybody, got Davin slow hot in his shirt. But Davin was a politician like the senator. He wouldn't ever cross an issue straight off, for chance of losing it entirely before he figured a way of approach. But he'd talk right steady while he was thinking—to throw you off the argument.

Davin said, "The boys tell me we got a new commanding officer here in Harper's Ferry. Just come up from Richmond to take over. Had a meeting of all the militia gin'rals yesterday and whittled 'em down to army size. They all come out of meeting captains and under. Those that come out at all. Only old Cap'n Murt couldn't go to th' meetin' on account he was sleepin' off a jug. So I guess he's still a gin'ral. Only one left, though," and Davin went on eating roast hog.

Forney Manigault hadn't taken his eyes off Roan the whole time. Nor Roan his.

"And another thing," Forney said. "These yere hogs, Roan. You buying them out of yore barrel-lifting bet money?"

"I wasn't," Roan said. "Does that bother yore appetitie?"

"Not buyin'," said Forney, "is stealin'."

Davin said, "The new man's name is Colonel Tom Jackson from down the Institute at Lexington. Taught school there." As he said that, he was sort of looking up over Roan's head at something behind, and he looked so long, everybody else turned slow around to see what he was looking at, and there stood a tall stranger, better than six feet, in a plain blue uniform coat, sort of frayed and shiny at the sleeves, with an Institute cap tilted so's not to hide his eyes. Talk of Catlett eyes—the eyes in that man's head you'd never forget, once you looked into them. Like blue lights. There's killing in Catlett eyes and there was killing in this man's eyes, too, but it was deep down under his kindness. Controlled, so's anger'd have to go clear to the bottom of his soul to bring it up.

Davin got up on his feet. "Honored to have you jine us at breakfast, suh."

"Thank you kindly. I'm Colonel Jackson." The man nodded. "What company is this?"

Cap Murt came out of the bushes just then, buttoning his frock coat from Mexico over his pants and hooking on his old artillery sword. Cap Murt was crowding seventy and his eyes weren't so good.

He skirted around the boys and walked up to this Colonel Jackson close enough to see the eagles on his coat, and he said, "Good morning to you, colonel. Brigadier Gin'ral Murtagh Patton, commandin' the Short Mountain Light Cav'ry Brigade. What can I do for you, sir?" Then something came between those two like a twig cracking. For a moment they stood stump still, before Cap'n Murt threw back his head like an old bull and roared, "Good Lord in heaven, effen it ain't Lootinint Jackson from the Chapultepec Road!" and he saluted. "Sarjint Patton, sir, of Magruder's Battery. That was my gun you and me man-hauled acrost the ditch!"

This Colonel Jackson smiled. It came into his eyes like a glory, and it wrapped around him and ole Murt until they were a million miles away in their memories. And the colonel held out his hand.

"Sergeant Patton!" he said, and he chuckled. "Did you ever find out where the Fourteenth Infantry got to that day?"

"No, sir. Never did." Cap shook his head, tears in his eyes from remembering. "I was too plumb wore out to go look for 'em. All I could do was to serve that gun with you. We was droppin' round shot in the hip pockets of them Mexicans shortly! I guess we kinda won that war, eh, lootinint?"

General Jackson laughed. It doesn't sound right to call him colonel even if he was only a colonel there at Harper's Ferry. "Our part of it anyway, sergeant. I'm going to need a good man like you at headquarters. An old regular," he said. "We've got to make an army out of these volunteers."

Cap said, "Any time you say. Any place. You jine us now for breakfast, sir? Honored to have you."

"I've had my breakfast, thank you. Looks like a very fine mess of roast pig you have here," and he shot a look over toward the bushes where the hide and the leavings were. "Chester White, from the hide. The commissary issue you that?"

"Well, not exactly, sir," Cap said. "It comes under the heading of supplementary field rations, I should put it. If I had to report it in writin'."

"I see," General Jackson nodded. "Some members of the Maryland Legislature visited camp yesterday and one of them mentioned that the country north of the Potomac was excellent breeding ground for Chester Whites. He said that a farmer named Satterlee had a herd of several hundred."

Davin Ancrum was taken with General Jackson's friendly manner. "Yes, sir. That's right, sir," he said. "Twelve miles around South Mountain. Up near Burkittsville."

"Is that so?" The general looked at him.

That's when Roan stepped in front of Davin and said, "If there's blame, I'm taking that blame, sir. All of it."

"What blame would that be?" The general raised his eyebrows.

"For foraging the hog, sir. Stealing it—if that's to be the word. And four other hogs before this one."

General Jackson thought it out for a minute, then he said, "There are a lot of technicalities in a war. For instance, if this hog was rooting in Pennsylvania when you appropriated it, we could call that foraging, for it would be property in the enemy's country. Its being a Maryland hog, however—makes a slight difference. Maryland is still trying to make up her mind whether to join the Confederacy or not. So, until she decides, there is a possibility that Mr. Satterlee's hogs are loyal Southern hogs—and to take them without paying for them would be stealing." Right up to that last it was as if he were a schoolteacher trying to explain a point. And Roan took it that way, first on one foot, then on the other. But when the general said "loyal Southern hogs" there was quiet fun in it suddenly, lurking there just under the surface of the words—a smile in the eyes alone. "At least," he said, "that is how the Maryland senator put it to me when he lodged Mr. Satterlee's complaint."

"Yes, sir," Roan said. "It won't happen again."

When General Jackson went on to the next camp, inspecting, ole Cap cut up his extra red flannel underpants and made himself the biggest set of artillery sergeant's chevrons ever. He sewed them on his coat sleeves and took the feathers out of his cap.

"Now," he said, "that Lootinint Jackson's promoted me up to headquarters, y'all goin' to see some changes made around here."

First thing happened we got a drill schedule and all the separate companies got regimented up together. When the horns blew now, you got up. You ate. You drilled. You went to sleep.

Then General Jackson got the trains working so that his army could sleep at night. He wrote a letter to the president of the Baltimore and Ohio Rail Road asking him to please run all the heavy coal trains on the eastbound track through Harper's Ferry between eleven and one o'clock in the daytime. Cap'n Murt was in charge of paper work at headquarters by that time. That's how the company knew why the night coal trains stopped.

There'd been a coolness between Roan and Forney Manigault ever since that first day the general stopped by camp. Because Roan had pretty nearly got young Davin into trouble. When the eastbound coal trains stopped rumbling through at night, Forney said, "When y'goin' to do what Gin'ral Jackson told you to do, Roan?"

Roan looked at him full. "What'd he tell?"

"Plain as speaking out, he said you stole those five Chester Whites. When y'goin' to ride up to Satterlee's and pay him?"

Roan said, "How far back in the Manigault family they breed this hoss thief—y'all have to be so all-fired honest out in public about everything since?"

Young Davin Ancrum was standin' there quiet until the horse-thief part. Then he eased into the talk like the senator.

"Speaking of hosses, I got to get Old Nell back home by June. If I don't get me a Yankee hoss by then, I got to go for a foot soldier and walk this yere war!"

Forney said, "Roan, I don't take talk against the Manigault family. If y'll step down to the river bank, suh, I'll be pleased to have my satisfaction."

Now, Roan was big and there wasn't any question that he could jasperoo Forney. But Roan was a gentleman. He never fought men he was sure he could take. He said, "Forney, I spoke in lightness. If it appeared insultin' to you, I apologize. I figure ten dollars a hog. I got forty dollars in bets from lifting hogsheads with my teeth from the Second, Fourth, Fifth and Twenty-Seventh Virginians—with ten more to go from the Thirty-third after recall tonight. It was to be for buying Davin here a hoss, but if you think Gin'ral Jackson wants those hogs paid for, I'll pay. For I ain't never seen a man like Ole Blue Light. You just have to do what he wants. Ask or not."

Forney nodded. "I'm glad to hear you say that, Roan, and to show you my talk ain't just empty preacher talk, heah"—and he handed Roan a wad of paper money. "Everybody in the comp'ny ate on them five Chester Whites, so I took up a collection of two-fifty apiece. Add yore own two-fifty and you've got fifty dollars for Satterlee, with yore barrel-liftin' fifty still left for Davin's new hoss."

Davin said, "That's right friendly of you, Roan, to want to buy me a hoss. I ain't going to need the courtesy, though, I get a sight of some hoss-ridin' Yankees."

But you couldn't walk in and out of camp nowadays when the prowling itch was on you at night. General Jackson had fellas at night with guns on the covered bridge and the canal bridge and the roads out west and south. They challenged. And you couldn't get a pass to go out either. You just plain couldn't go out, so those hogs wouldn't have been paid for to this day if it hadn't been for that railroad deal. The coal trains were all going down to Washington noontime for three or four days, but the empties had to come up at night and they were almost as noisy. So General Jackson wrote another letter to the railroad president, Cap told, and suggested that he hold the empties overnight in Washington one night, and send 'em up west again on the other track between eleven and one in the daytime, so that all the cars would be rumbling each way through Harper's Ferry during the same two hours. Then he sent the 5th Virginia Infantry, Colonel Harper, west to Martinsburg to see the suggestion was carried out properly, and he sent a detachment east to Point o' Rocks, including the Short Mountain Cavalry, for the same reason. The night the company got down there, Roan, Forney and Davin took off to pay old Satterlee back for his five Chester White hogs.

When they turned left off the Frederick road, Davin said, "We're making good time. You don't suppose we could push on a ways toward Chambersburg to have a try at getting a Yankee soldier's hoss for me, do you?"

"Leave well enough be," Forney said. "There's twelve thousand Yankees in Chambersburg."

"That's what I mean," Davin said. "We're sure to get one good hoss among that many."

Roan was riding a little ahead off the crown of the road. He pulled up, listening with his head turned sideways to what little night wind there was.

"What you hear, Roan?"

He shook his head he didn't know, and flatted his hand for the two to stand while he rode up under the rise like General Jackson taught in the drill.

Forney unslung his rifle, and Davin, seeing him do it, unslung his, too, and they sat there stiff in their saddles, waiting. Pretty soon Roan came back, his own rifle across his pommel.

"There's twenty wagons in front of Satterlee's, standin' there headed this way. And there's lantern light and some fellas on hossback. Loadin' pens are full of hogs.... Davin, you hold our hosses. Forney and me're goin' down for a close look."

They went down on foot, keeping off the road, and they skirted wide to come in mid-column of the wagon convoy. They were commissary wagons with U. S. on the canvas, half of them loaded with Chester Whites already and the other half loading. Three, four hundred hogs, all prime. There was a soldier counting tally by lantern and another with a sword standing by to give orders. Four others supervising Satterlee's men's loading. Counting one waggoner for each wagon, twenty-six Yankees all told.

Lying in the ditch opposite, Roan pulled a spear of sweetgrass and bit his teeth on it for the juice, looking and listening. Forney was hunkered down beside him, thinking and gnawing his long upper lip like he does.

Then he whispered, "It's sure enough Yankee soldiers loadin' them hogs. Buy or steal for them, it's foragin' for us if we take 'em now." Just like the judge handing down a considered opinion. Roan touched his shoulder and they started back up to where Davin was with the horses, and told him.

"Gentlemen, let's take them hogs," Davin said.

"The thought was in my mind," Roan said, "except with odds of nine to one, it's prob'ly goin' to mean some shootin' and I don't aim to get you hurt, Davin."

"Mr. Catlett, suh," Davin said, "I'll thank you to leave m'tender years out of this. If I'm man enough to carry a gun in war, I'm man enough to shoot a Yankee. That bein' settled, what's yore plan?"

Roan grinned. "It's a simple plan," he said. "An inferior force only has one chance for success. Attack with surprise—like Gin'ral Jackson teaches. Them six hossback soldiers are goin' to ride ahead when they start. Davin and I are goin' to make 'em turn right on the Frederick road for Point o' Rocks, instead of left, and ride on with 'em.... Forney, yo're goin' to stay at the crossroads t'see that each hog wagon turns and follows on. Then you bring up the rear to keep the convoy closed up."

Forney said, "I reckon that covers it, Roan."

Roan kneed his horse. "If yo're ready, gentlemen, we'll take positions for openin' the ball"—and he nodded back to where they could hear the whips begin to crack and the wheels to creak—"for the fiddles're tunin' up."

They moved on back to the Frederick-road junction and took up position this side on the road to Satterlee's, in shadow under a clump of trees.

After a while Roan whispered soft, "I ain't never killed a man, so I don't know how it'll be. Neither do you two. But if it'll help y'all to think it out, I'm goin' to kill the first Yankee tonight who don't do what I say, when I say it. It ain't goin' to be me personally. It's goin' to be me as a soldier of the sovereign state of Virginia, which was a dominion in its own right long before the states was made united."

"Thanks, Roan," Davin said. "That's right comfortable thinkin'."

Forney just sat his horse, deep drawn in his own mind. Then the first wagon topped the rise, moving at the walk, and the soldier with the sword was up ahead with the five other horse soldiers, free of the high-rising dust, and about ten yards between them and that first wagon. Roan let them just pass him. Then he kneed in behind, between them and the leading wagon.

"Turn right, gentlemen! And don't reach for yore hand guns!" He had his own out, held close in with the hammer cocked full.

You could see the whites of their eyes like swamp mallow blobbing the darkness as the Yankee detail whipped around to see who was talking. There was the space of half a drawn breath, then from orderly two by two the horses were up, pirouetted, kneed out of line, the men cursing and reaching. Roan shot close, fast. Twice. And twice—and twice again the echoes came back down the Valley so perfect it was almost as if that was what he'd done it for—to hear the echo. For that's the way a man thinks at times like that, apart from it all. Not quite living it at the time. Not seeing Roan barrel-whip the fifth man off his horse and wrist-lock the sword man into an arm bar in the saddle. "Ah said don't reach, suh!"

And Davin with his rifle in the face of Number One Waggoner, "You heard what Mistuh Catlett tole you! Turn right and don't draw!" But what you never forget are the belly screams torn from deep pain. Blood choking a man's breathing like mud clogging a pump, and somebody sobbing like a baby while his legs thrash the ditch weeds.

"Lord A'mighty," the sword man yelled, "what is this—a holdup? Leggo my arm!"

"This yere's Gin'ral Jackson's army, suh! Yo're a pris'ner of war—and all yore hogs with you! Turn right, I said, and git!"

With that, the head wagon started and turned right, and you could hear Forney galloping rear and turning the rest of them. "Never mind that shootin'! Jest follow the wagon ahead and keep goin'!"

It was that easy—only it wasn't, for Roan. He knew he'd killed, and the feeling was fresh in his mind, like a smashed finger hurting all up his shoulder in spite of what he'd said before. He rode to one side, keeping the sword man ahead of him and the lead waggoner in the corner of his eye. And he grew up a mite that night. Grew a mite hard inside. The fun was gone out of it, and it never would come back full blown like it had been, for blood was in it now. And dead men. But pretty soon it got plain spoken in Roan's mind. It's when you're born, that does it to you. There was Braddock, years ago, cut to pieces by the Indians in spite of what Colonel Washin'ton told him. Then there was the British to fight and lick down Yorktown way, and Roan could remember his own grandpappy telling how they did that. And there was Cap'n Murt at Chapultepec with Colonel Jackson. And himself on the Point o' Rocks road tonight. It's when you're born. If you're born to a war—fight it! And when you fight-fight for keeps.

Then Roan missed Davin, and he shouted, and Davin didn't answer. He shouted for Forney, and Forney didn't answer, and the cold worms crawled in his stomach, for he could see the tree holes now in the false light with dawn to come just beyond. He kneed out to the roadside and looked back into the wagon dust that hung low in the morning damp, like brush-fire smoke. The hogs were beginning to squeal, for it was getting on to their slopping time. One wagonload would take it up from the next, until all three hundred were giving out like the low notes of those coal-burning steam calliopes on Market Day. "Davin!"—and that time Davin came up through the dust, galloping. "Where's Forney?"

Davin reined in beside Roan and shook his head. "Them danged honest Manigaults!" he said. "Forney rode all the way back to Satterlee's after we got the wagons turned—to pay him for the five hogs we stole. And you know what Satterlee said? He said he sold these hogs to the Yankees for twenty dollars a head. 'In that case,' says Forney, 'for ten dollars a head you'll be pleased to know five of your hogs have been loyal to the Confederacy,' and he threw fifty dollars paper at his feet. Then he drew on Satterlee and he said, 'Yankee money's contraband of war, suh. And if you've got it for tradin' with the enemy, yo're enemy too. So hand it ovah!' " Davin jerked his thumb. "Forney's ridin' at the rear with six thousand dollars gold notes in his pants and his conscience clear."

"How'd you git blood on yore shirt?" Roan asked him.

"You shot me, Mistuh Catlett."

"I what?"

"Mistuh Catlett, yo're the best shot in the county, hand gun or rifle. But you shot me, suh."

"How d'you mean—I shot you?"

"Like I said." Davin grinned. "The first Yankee you killed— was me, suh. You creased off my upper arm. Missed clean the bone, but by deflection the lead took the Yankee in the throat after it nicked me. Nervous, I reckon you were, Mistuh Catlett. Would you like that story to get around the comp'ny, suh?"

"Not to Forney, I wouldn't. Nor to yore pappy, Davin."

"Quite so, Mistuh Catlett." Davin bowed in the saddle. "The wound then becomes an hon'ble war wound, suh, provided there's a little less talk about my tendah age and how I have to do what you say, place of m'father. But militarily speakin', suh, I'd be pleased to follow you through the windows of hell into the back yard and over the fence any time you've a mind. I got five good hosses out of last night's fracas—to pick my choice of, come full light!"

It was broad day when the hog convoy came into Point o' Rocks. Broad day and better. Nearer half past ten when they got in. The up trains for the eleven-to-one-o'clock shuttle through Harper's Ferry were lined up, head to tail, on the westbound tracks, waiting for the word. A solid mess of cars as far up the tracks as you could see, and over by the telegraph office there was General Jackson himself with Cap'n Murt. The operator came out with a telegraph form.

Cap'n read it. "Colonel Harper at Martinsburg, sir," he said. "His eastbound trains will be all marshaled off the single line onto the double line in about fifteen more minutes."

General Jackson nodded. Then he looked up and saw those twenty Yankee commissary wagons full of hogs, with Roan and Davin and Forney riding the line of them to a halt.

"Come here, sir," he called to Roan. "You're the Chester White man, aren't you? Where'd you get those wagons?"

"If there's any blame, sir, I'll take it"—and Roan told him the story.

General Jackson turned away once or twice and ran his hand down his nose and over his beard. Finally he said, "Well, sir, from our standpoint, the night's been right profitable. We could use wagons and we could use pork. And six thousand dollars in gold notes'd help the war chest in Richmond. But I don't doubt in the least that Mr. Satterlee's got another complaint. And he'll make it noisy this time. So drive the wagons up the platform ramp and load them on the empty flatcars."

"Yo're not sending them back, suh?" Roan gasped.

General Jackson just looked at him full in the eyes and ignored the question like it had never been asked. Cold. Then he walked a few paces up the platform.

"Roan," old Cap Murt said soft, "don't never mistake again— an' ask Colonel Jackson what he's goin' to do in a war. He don't even tell his chief of the staff, an' all he writes his missus is how nice the roses smell outside headquarters. Besides, he's busy this morning. Once he gets all the Balt-O cars and engines on these two double tracks, he's switching the whole caboodle of it onto the branch line south to run it to Winchester and horse-draw it from there over to the Manassas Gap Rail Road at Strasburg. The Confed'racy needs cars and engines, too, as well as hogs and wagons."

Roan Catlett stared across at General Jackson. The general was turning to pace back the platform. When he came to Roan again, the glory was in his eyes. "When you forage, youngster," he said quietly, "forage." Then he smiled and Roan's guts sort of melted and ran down inside his legs and, from that moment on, it was, in a way, like love for a woman in him for Stonewall Jackson—a part of himself gone for all the rest of his life, leaving him empty and grateful and humble of soul inside. General Jackson saw it there, for those things show plain and they leave a man naked, and it isn't good for others to see. So he put his hand on Roan's shoulder and he said, "And what time is breakfast this morning, Corporal Catlett—if the invitation still holds?"

The Potomac River then became the focal point of war. Washington, where the crawling forces of the Union were concentrating, lay north of it with the broad sweep of Virginia to the southward. All that spring patrols denied the right to cross in freedom. Men died in small actions, whetting their angering souls for the full-bladed slaughter of the greater fights to come. To the westward the long arc of the river lay across the entrance to the rich food treasury of the Shenandoah Valley and Lieutenant Colonel J. E. B. Stuart became the watchdog. To the eastward the river was the barricade before the Capital, manned by the swarming volunteers of McDowell.

It was to be a short war. All wars are, at their beginnings. Two great armies were in concentration, great in numbers for that day, but grotesque in ill-discipline, heterogeneous in equipment, plagued with unqualified officers. They grew as cancer grows, their size increasing their threat and decreasing any possibility of close control. They were two vast concentrations of rabble under arms. Little more. Some of the officers on both sides were career officers, but pitifully few compared to the total. Again, the professional horizons of the regulars were the small horizons of garrison duty and frontier service. None of them had seen troop concentrations of this size before, or had any experience of administration or command or sanitation of large forces.

In this respect, both gathering forces were about equal. They were equal in respect to lack of and non-uniformity of equipment. And they were equal in a hotheaded will to fight—the questionable and uninitiated will to fight that is based upon no previous experience in the actuality of battle. Each army believed fully *that once joined in combat with the other it would sweep the field clean. Recruit vinegar, you might say. But there was more to it than that; this was one war in history wherein the men on both sides knew what they were fighting for from the very beginning, for it had taken thirty years to bring the disagreement to the field. Their heritage was common. In unity they had fought the Indian and pushed their colonies west of the Appalachians across the central plains to the Pacific paradise of California. Twice together they had fought the British off their fledgling necks. Together, they had subjugated Mexico and dictated peace deep in the heart of the Mexican homeland.*

Now this unity was shattered and it was shattered on one basic point of disagreement. Did or did not each individual state that had held the power to enter into coalition with the others, still retain the power to withdraw? Could a contracting power enter into national union by its own sovereign will and still retain enough of that will to withdraw when displeased with national majority decisions? In other words, how far were the sacred minority privileges of American thinking to go—so far that the union of the country itself could be destroyed by them?

Slavery of the black man was convenient propaganda—glib words for shallow thinking. Johnnie Reb and Damyankee were the slogans. But the fact of the matter lay in states' rights as against the authority those states had given to the federal government and now sought to withhold. McDowell's army represented the federal police power. Beauregard stood in defense of man's primary allegiance to his state. That was the issue.

So then while two great armies sprawled across the face of the Potomac country, growling at each other, the men of those armies grew slightly older in their minds. The pageantry and bright adventure of the march away were gone from it, the fluttering handkerchiefs of the girls, the last solemn words of paternal wisdom, the silent tears of mother heart.

They had killed and been killed and a blue coat and a gray coat were the symbols of mounting hatred. They had buried boys they had gone to school with a few months before, shot it out in picket actions and skirmishes with other boys who had been reading Caesar's Commentaries in Boston in March while they read them in Richmond.

So they moved toward First Manassas—First Bull Run, whichever you please—for the first great trial of strength. Here they would fight a dreadful battle that would cloud the heavy summer air with the sick sweet stench of decomposing flesh for weeks afterward. There would be men on both sides who could never see the full yellow moon again without the grease of gangrene clogging their nostrils through the associative channels of memory.

Equal in strength and training, with equally commendable tactical plans, the two armies would meet, and the tide of battle would join full and deadlock for a time. Then subtly it would turn in the Southern favor for no good or known reason unless it was Stonewall Jackson's counterattack from the Henry Hill. The Northern Army would break and in the inertia of indiscipline flee toward Washington, its officers in many instances getting there ahead of their men—before the taverns could be drunk dry. By the same indiscipline, Beauregard's Southerners would fail to exploit their God-given opportunity to pursue, fail to push the advantage of victory. Had they done so, Washington would have fallen and history would have had a different face. Of what nature, who can say?

But the important thing was what that battle did to men's minds. It coerced blind hatred into the beginnings of mutual respect. These were foemen worthy of each other's steel. Win, lose, or draw this was a breed of men who could not deny each other. Let the New York politicians curse the Johnnie Rebs for defaulting cutthroats. Let the Richmond staff colonels damn the Yankees for ravishers of Southern womanhood, but no combat soldier on either side at Manassas ever hated blindly again.

For Manassas was the birthplace of a nation, two lifetimes distant from Valley Forge—a rebirth in steel and blood of those principles that freemen find more necessary to defend than life itself, the right to political integrity in principle and fact.

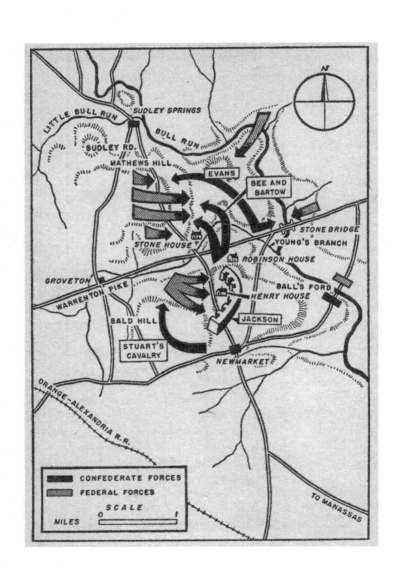

STUART'S CHARGE
AT BULL RUN

THIS SOUP TUREEN of the Washington family was a lovely thing. Pale cream salt glaze with raised blue cornflowers in delicate clusters. You could see the shadow of your finger through it, held to the light. One of the earlier Washingtons, before President George, had the soup tureen about 1760 from Josiah Wedgwood himself, of Stoke-upon-Trent.

That was all in the letter from Forney Manigault's grandmother. It was early in June they organized the 1st Brigade of the Army of the Shenandoah and General Jackson was given command of it. The Short Mountain Cavalry Company was attached to it; so was the Reverend Doctor Pendleton's artillery battery with their four old smooth-bores, called Matthew, Mark, Luke and John. That's the way they gave the orders, too: "Stand by, Matthew.... Matthew, read-ay?...Fire, Matthew!" "Gospel on the way, sir."

Roan Catlett was detailed to brigade headquarters riding dispatch during the Falling Waters skirmish, because he was orderly in his dress and habits for a youngster. He wasn't twelve feet from General Jackson when a Yankee cannon ball tore a limb off a tree. General Jackson was writing out an order. He brushed the splinters off the paper and clawed them out of his beard and went on writing without even looking up.

Just after that cannon ball missed, old Doctor Latham drove up the road with the soup tureen and the letter, watching the battle, curious, through his spectacles, like he was on a round of calls and getting the news to talk it. Forney Manigault was over on the far left flank with the company, fending. The doctor haltered his horse and rig to a fence rail. He saw Roan and he said, "Come yere, Roan," and he told it to Roan about the soup tureen Forney's grandmother had sent with the letter to Forney's Great-Aunt Chastity. He had a package of other letters from home for all the boys in the Short Mountain Company and a quart bottle of sulphur and molasses for Davin Ancrum, 'count of Davin was only turned fifteen, and still a growing boy, and his mother wanted him to take it for spring toning.

There were leaves falling from the trees. The old doc looked up. "That's mighty odd, leaves falling in July, Roan. Don't recall ever having seen that before."

"No, sir. No, sir," Roan said. "Bullets cuttin' them, sir. Mebbe you better move the rig down the road a piece, sir. We're kinda close in here."

"Nonsense," doc told him. "Can't see down there. You go on about your business, Roan. I'll just sit here a spell and watch."

So Roan took the letters and the soup tureen, and he said, "Yes, sir. Yes, sir," and all the rest of the fight he was worried sick to retching for fear a bullet'd smash that beautiful piece of Wedgwood china before he could get it over to Forney.

Forney was pretty shaken when he saw Roan, because the first boy in the company was killed that day. Hadley Stuart. Hadley was lying roadside with his hands dirty. That's what you thought of first—even when you saw the throat shot clean out of him. *Let's wash his hands clean.* Lying there with the summer breeze moving his fine blond hair, like he was still alive—only gray in the face and chiseled sharp like a statue and lying awful flat to the ground. You couldn't believe it was laughing Hadley.

"Ridin' right beside me, Roan," Forney whispered. "I heard it hit him—like a rock chunked in swamp mud," and young Davin Ancrum just stood there with the tears running down his own dirty face.

All you could think of was the news getting home to the Stuart place—how Hadley was killed in the fight and his laughter gone down the summer wind. With his mother, after a while, asking, soft, with the desperation held tight in her, "Was his face hurt? Hadley was such a pretty baby."

"It's an omen to me, Roan." Forney shook his head. "Just a few inches left and it'd been me. Maybe it will be, next time."

"Stop it!" Roan's voice was quiet. "We got to bury. Hadley's ours. We don't let nobody touch ours but us. There—by the sycamore, where it's peaceful like.... Forney, this yere's George Washin'ton's soup tureen yore grandmother sent for you to take to yore Aunt Chastity over Manassas way.... Davin, this yere's yore sulphur-and-molasses tonic."

About two weeks later it was, along in July, when the Short Mountain Cavalry Company was ordered up near Shepherdstown to join Lt. Col. James Ewell Brown Stuart's regiment. That was the fellow they got to calling "Jeb" Stuart later along, you may remember. He was a right personable man, of medium height, built in one powerful piece of grown manhood—to sit a horse and nothing else. He'd been out on the prairies Indian-fighting and they said he knew every name of his three hundred sabers, and each squad he sent out on scout he instructed personally, each man by name. Close-knit and blackhaired, Colonel Stuart, with an arrogant West Point eye to him, but it had a pixy smile deep in it that they said the ladies went for mighty easy.

He looked the company over when it reported to him, and when he got to Forney Manigault he said, "What's that gunny bag hanging to your cantle, soldier?" and Forney said, "That's George Washin'ton's soup tureen, sir."

Stuart looked full into Forney's eyes for insolence, but he didn't find any.

"How'd you come by it?" he said.

Forney sort of shifted a bit under Stuart's eyes. "Well, sir," Forney said, "my grandmother inherited it from the Custises and she always promised, when she died it was to go to Aunt Chastity, over Manassas way. Well, sir, she knows I'm to the wars and she writes how some very old friend of hers named General Beauregard is over Manassas way getting set to fight this Yankee General McDowell around Washin'ton. She figures that with all them hundred thousand Yankees, General Beauregard's goin' to need some help from General Jackson's Valley Brigade up here—and that I'd get to go over when they send for us. That's about the how of it, sir. I got it wrapped against breaking—in m'extra drawers—but it worries me pretty much."

Then, before Colonel Stuart could answer, young Davin Ancrum, on Forney's off side, said, "A fine old lady, Forney's grandmother, sir. I got the cover to her tureen in my cantle pack to keep the two parts from smashing together at the gallop, but I'll sure be glad to get it to where it's goin'. How soon you aim to start for Manassas, sir?"

You could see Colonel Stuart was having trouble with the dignity a colonel has to have.

"My respects to your grandmother, young man, but General Beauregard has not given me his confidence to the extent that she seems to enjoy it."

Right then an orderly galloped in, looking for Lieutenant Colonel Stuart, and after Stuart read the orders, he looked at Forney sort of funny this time, and he said, "I'd like to meet your grandmother someday, sir. I've got a place for her on my staff."

The Valley Brigade slipped out the sixty-odd miles for Manassas behind a cavalry screen. It marched from Winchester east, forded the Shenandoah, waist deep, and came down out of the Blue Ridge through Ashby's Gap to Piedmont, to take the steam cars on from there. It was getting hot, July hot, when dawn lies in the valleys in thick blue haze and you can still smell yesterday's sun scorch like cindered toast. Coming through Manassas Junction before light, the column got a halt order passed down through it, and that stopped the Short Mountain Company so close to a hospital that you could hear a man screaming. Not conscious screaming that you can control, but deep out of delirium. Some poor devil wounded in the skirmish around the Stone Bridge on the eighteenth. In the last dark of night, that's not good to hear.

When Roan spoke Forney in passing, Forney didn't answer. He just stood there in the dark, looking, like a strange face at the window. Roan turned and came back to him.

He said soft, "You let up, Forney, you hear? Thinking ahead is like punishing yoreself before you do wrong."

Forney just reached into his jacket. "I want you to see my father gets this letter afterwards. He's a family-thinking man. Proud of blood. He's got a right to know I tried." Forney shook his head. "Oh, it ain't anything in the letter but chat and news to him. I just kinda wanted to talk to him once more. Just let him get that—and you write him."

Roan took the letter. He held it a minute in both hands. "All right, Forney," and he bowed slightly, because that was the way with Roan.

Daylight broke about then, and along about six in the morning there was gunfire a little west of north, which folks said would be up around the Stone Bridge on the Warrenton Pike about six miles. So the brigades got on the road again—General Jackson's, Bee's and Bartow's—to march toward the gun fight. Bee and Bartow led off up the road that parallels the Orange and Alexandria Rail Road, with General Jackson's five Virginia infantry regiments trailing in the dust behind. And that was dust. It got seven, eight inches deep underfoot to walk in and two inches thick to breathe. At the road to Mitchell's Ford, the three brigades turned off left for due north, and about a mile and a half north of the railroad and a straight mile south of Bull's Run from Mitchell's Ford, they halted. A right pretty place.

Sometime after nine the sound of that gun fight began to shift left. Sudley Springs by the sound now. When General

Jackson finished prayers, he put a glass over toward his left flank and he said, "That's low dust on the Sudley Road. Thick-clouded. Infantry, and it can't be ours. The Short Mountain Company will move out until it contacts Colonel Stuart's regiment. Bring me back his word on the situation at the gallop. You'll find him between the Henry Farm House and the Stone Bridge, probably behind the ridge line." That was General Jackson—he could see through the hills.

Roan led 'cross country north and west. He'd lost his hat, and the sun brought the dark red out of his black hair like slow embers in charcoal. Forney, with that Wedgwood soup tureen in the gunny bag from his cantle, rode next to Roan, quiet in his own thinking, with his cousin Davin watching him close and not liking what he saw in Forney's face.

About two miles on the way, there was a quick wind shift, like a fire swirl of smoke, and with it a retching stench from a draw. And there it was to ride through, with the horses blithering at it and some of the boys vomiting. The surgeons had used the place after the eighteenth, like they'd gone mad with the butcher knife. The horses were walking in it. A green hand clawing at their hoofs with half an arm on it and a couple of smashed feet lying side by side in shoes, with ten inches of leg, but no man on them. The greasy flies clouded thick, and there was a field rat!

Roan lashed through that mess. "Git that off yore minds, y'hear?" But how could you?

Through his tight-shut teeth, Forney said, "If I git hit bad for the surgeons to carve me, don't take my hand gun off me, Roan! Let me keep it—for out."

Roan turned slow in the saddle with the light of those Catlett eyes of his burning deep into Forney. "That's three times, Mr. Manigault," he said, soft. "Have quit of that kind of talk!"

"There's Colonel Stuart!" Davin pointed, and it was. He had left his regiment and ridden over to the Henry Hill when the battle shifted. At fifty-yard intervals back, he had his connecting files waiting, so he could shout and the word'd pass like telegraph.

Across the pike the Yankees were pouring down thick between Mr. Mathews' House and the old Stone House, heading to force over Young's Branch, like ripe blueberries dumped from a broken-wheeled market cart. There were artillery shells puffing like cotton swabs close over their heads with red in them, like cracked frosted knuckles. It didn't look actual, though. That was the funny thing. It looked like a picture drawing in a schoolbook.

The worst thing was the sight of that flag with them. The right of that was hard to come by. That was the old glory flag of long back. It had blood in its red stripes from Roan's own grandpappy's veins—and Davin's great-uncle. It had honor in its white from the whole Manigault tribe from long gone. One of those stars in the blue was for the sovereign state of Virginia herself. But there it was across the valley—with the damn Yankees having hold of it. And how can you think that out? It puts the bitter tears deep. So deep you can't cry them. In Davin Ancrum's boy's mind it went; *I git the chance, I'm goin' to shoot me a blue-bellied color sergeant and git my flag back.* All in a moment, which is battle too. Thoughts for a lifetime that take twenty seconds.

When Roan brought the point up to report to Colonel Stuart at his lookout, the colonel said, "Tell General Jackson we have two enemy divisions on our left flank, I believe." Then he pointed down to our line in front. "Fending along out there in the corn is Colonel Evans' riflemen with the Louisiana Tigers. Cooke and Wade Hampton are backing him up, but it isn't going to be enough against this flanking move. I don't think you'll need to tell him." Stuart nodded behind where they were and a shade over his left shoulder. There was General Bartow's Brigade coming up on the run, yelling, with Imboden's battery galloping like the devil before breakfast. And on the other side this General Bee with his Carolina fireballs screaming to drink blood hot from a boot, without sugar or cream.

But what Jeb Stuart was really nodding at was General Jackson. Those two knew how to make the land fight for them. That's West Point, and it's a knack precious few generals ever learn. If the land don't fight for you, soldiers die.

The fight below wasn't all together. It was meeting the Yankee force piecemeal—first Evans, next Cooke, then Bartow, and then Bee and Hampton. Punch, hit or miss, and after a while all of 'em falling back. Getting snakewhipped now, sure enough.

Jackson alone wasn't sucked in. That's what Stuart really meant when he nodded. Jackson had the 1st Brigade coming up slow, like on drill, and taking position with the hill crest to shelter them. You saw him and saw the line below breaking up and falling back, and it was like Christmas, when you know you're not going to get what you want.

That was when there was a clear close sound as if a sharp-honed razor caught the strop and sliced right through it. Forney Manigault looked down. His left foot was still holding the stirrup on his boot toe, but the stirrup leather was trailing the dust, cut clean in two by a bullet.

Roan Catlett grinned. "That's one, Forney," he said, "and you lived through it. What for you had to call it twice more on yourself?"

Nobody knows where time goes. It was ten minutes ago the company went to find Stuart, just after nine o'clock, and now it was crowding for noon by the sun. There was a right smart mill for a time around the Henry House below, and Imboden's battery was galloping back up, everybody shouting. Then our infantry was breaking its line all along, and fighting up backwards, shooting from the knee. There were some powerful wide gaps in it, like kicked-out teeth, and the men sure looked jasperooed. Through the smoke and right in the front of it all, there was this madman galloping his soaped horse, waving his sword. And you could hear. "Look!" he shouted. "There is Jackson——" They said it was General Bee from Carolina. Then General Jackson let loose on the battle, like a mountain man stepping up to mark in a Thanksgiving turkey shoot. His horse had been wounded, he had a big bullet tear in his coat at the hip and a bloody handkerchief wrapped around the broken middle finger of his left hand, but he looked like a man setting off late for church, mad because he wanted to get there before first hymn.

Now you can feel a battle turn. It don't make any difference how, for you ain't human in a battle. And nothing happens that's human. It just happens. As soon as the Shenandoah Brigade opened, that battle turned like a greased wheel, and the smile of God came upon General Jackson. He volleyed the whole Yankee army. Volleyed again, and the Yankee center buckled. Then the bayonets flashed on in the sunlight like a thousand shards of broken mirror, and General Jackson shouted, "If they're beating us, sir, we'll give them the bayonet!"

Forney yelled, "Roan, they got French soldiers down there!" and he whipped up his arm and pointed, and his hat snapped off and scaled away behind. He reached to his head like to catch it, and he turned slow around and stared at it, lying in the sumac with a hole through it.

Roan spat cotton that didn't clear his chin. "That's twice, Forney!"

They weren't French soldiers at all; they were what they called the New York Fire Zouaves, in red pants and caps with white leggings and pretty little blue short coats, coming off the Sudley Road. Column-of-fours.

Just as Forney pointed, a staff officer galloped up. "Colonel Stuart," he said, "General Beauregard directs that you bring your command into action at once and that you attack where the fighting is hottest!"

Colonel Stuart cupped his hands. "Boots and saddles!" and you could hear the repeat going back through his link files—an echo so fast it was like hail on a tin roof. In no time the head of Stuart's regimental column was coming up through the fences on Bald Hill at the trot with Capt. William Blackford leading. Stuart turned and waved the company into position in the column. Then he hand-signaled again for the rear to oblique left and deploy on right into line. It's a mighty pretty sight, horse and man, when the sabers flash and the trumpet shrieks. Only you've got scant chance to enjoy it, for a horse at the gallop does a hundred yards as fast as a steam train, when blood's in his nostrils. Halfway to them—those five hundred red pants faced around and leveled and fired a long streak of red flame in pale blue smoke. Capt. Welby Carter went down; then the smoke was too thick to see a thing. But they couldn't see either and in the battle fog they made their mistake. They reloaded instead of standing with the knife at charge bayonets. Half reloaded, Stuart hit them.

It was bloody awful. Half Stuart's horses thought they were hunting and that they were making to clear this red-pants fence with smoke over it, so they gathered and took off. Their fore hoofs topped into faces and chests. They caved like picked pumpkins, and the charge went through. The charge broke then and turned in a thrashing mill to smash back through the gouting shambles from the rear. It was awful. Sick, puking, stenching awful.

Roan was drenched in cold sweat. Forney had blood all the way to the shoulder. Young Davin Ancrum had only four inches of blade left. Snapped clean. He threw the stumped hilt back at them, like it was a rock.

"Bite on that!" he yelled, and other things.

In the galloping scramble to get uphill again, Forney shouted something and kneed left, pulling his mount crosswise to Davin and Roan. Roan yelled, "Not that way!" and there was a chunk sound and a muffled smash of breaking china, and Forney shrieked like a cut pig, "I'm hit, I'm hit!" Roan grabbed at him and got him over the hill still in the saddle.

Forney was hit all right. A calf's-ear nick through both sides of his rump. Only with the muscles stretched the way they were at the gallop, it looked like Forney'd got the whole bottom shot off him. They laid him over a log, face down, to plug lint in until it sopped up the blood. The girls down home sent lint to the company in perfumed-paper packages. You were supposed to guess which girl by the perfume. Roan took a pinch of lint and passed it in front of his nose like a pinch of snuff.

Then he plugged it into Forney and shook his head. "Forney, I'd be ashamed what yo're using this pore girl's petticoat for!"

"Shut up!" Forney grunted.

Roan took another pinch of lint and inhaled deep from it. "Forney," he said, "you called it three times on yourself. Maybe you better let God run his own war from now on."

"Shut up!" Forney grunted.

So Roan got the blood stopped and he rigged up a white shirt like a sort of diaper and he said, "Hold still while mamma pins you up, Forney."

You think it's funny? Well, it isn't. It's shock. It's what comes of fighting. Shock's gray like a casket cloth. Your soul's wrapped in it. You want to put your arms around somebody and cry like a baby. You get doing whatever—and you can't stop. Over and over until it leaves you.

Roan couldn't stop. "Dear Judge Manigault," he said, "I have a sad duty to perform in writing to you. Forney's been shot in th'——"

That was when Forney whipped up and spun on his heels, his boots sucking blood, and smashed Roan. Roan went down like a poleaxed ox, and there was Forney bawling like a toddler—real tears—crouched over Roan, his finger pointed rigid to the gunny bag at his cantle.

"Damn yore eyes, Roan Catlett!" he blubbered. "I broke my grandmother's soup tureen!" and he pressed both hands to his face with the sobs tearing out of him. "I heard it smash, damn you, Roan Catlett! I love my ole grandmother! She used to give me apples and take me walks and tell me stories!" And he sat down on the log with his head on his arms, and you'd thought his heart would break.

Davin Ancrum put his hand on Forney's shoulder. "Come on, Forney, don't take it so hard. I still got the cover whole."

Like a couple of old men sitting there, they were, nodding their heads solemnly and settling the affairs of the world.

"Yes"—Forney wiped his eyes—"that's right. We got the cover. Well," he said, "it's the best that I could do, but I'm sure sorry. Sure sorry." Roan opened his eyes. "Sure sorry, Roan," Forney said.

Roan got up. Probably didn't even know Forney'd hit him. Didn't act like it. Just said, "I got an idea you can sit sideways on a horse and get back to Manassas that way, Forney boy. Let's try."

Monday afternoon the whole company came back into Manassas, two by two, leading at the walk down the Union Mills Road. Feeling pretty good, because that Bull's Run battle was a jasperoo and General Jackson won it, for the Short Mountain money.

Sitting on a veranda of a house as you come into town, with a cushion to his chair and his polished boots cocked on the rail, was young Forney Manigault with a pipe of shag going.

"Well, well," said Forney. "My old friend Roan Catlett come from the wars," and he stood up and stretched a bit, elegant like.

An elderly gentleman came out of the house and squinted over his spectacles. "Yore friends, sir?" he said. "I'll have Commodus saddle yore charger.... Commodus!"

"Stand," Roan told the boys, "while we watch a passel of Negras get Mr. Manigault ready to accompany us."

Then the man's wife came out with doughnuts and lemonade. Lawyer and Mrs. Pemberton. Right-pleasant-spoken people. And it was all fun again, with one by one the company going in the big kitchen for a hot bath themselves and a change of shirt. Everybody laughing and telling how it was and how it was going to be now, with the war done and the Yankees gone home. Laughing, that is, until this macaroni rode up, with the carriage behind him in the street.

You've seen 'em in Richmond of a Sunday? Gray top hat with a high fresh collar to his ears and a folded silk neck cloth, black with small white dots. Gray frock coat and tight pants over his varnished half Wellingtons. Silver-knobbed crop and yellow gloves. It's all right if you like it, but as young as he was, about twenty-two, and right after a battle like Bull's Run—and on the finest horse you ever saw—it can rub you rough.

He signaled to the coachman to stop the carriage as if it mustn't come any closer with the princess in it. Then he took off his hat and he said, "I beg yore pardon, but can any of you tell me in what house the Carolinian General Bee's body lies?" Without the mannerly "sir" onto it.

Roan's eyes flicked. He straightened up slow and put his thumbs in his belt.

"Don't reckon that any of us here ever heard of any General Beesbody."

"Is that meant to be funny, suh?"

"It wasn't, sir," Roan told him, slow. "It's just the way you talk. I thought you said Beesbody. You slur your words, sir—for a Virginian."

"I am not a Virginian," and there was pond ice in it. "General Bee was killed—because of the Virginians," the fellow said in fury. "The word comes from Major Rhett direct. And Major Rhett is General Johnston's chief of staff, suh! He ought to know. In yesterday's battle the Carolinians bore the brunt. They were badly shaken. General Bee shouted for someone who calls himself General Jackson. 'Where is Jackson? Where is Jackson?' he shouted. To get him to come help him. But this Jackson didn't move an inch. He just stood where he was, not lifting a finger, like a"—the fellow's face was boiled scarlet—"like a damned stone wall!"

Roan took his thumbs out of his belt and dropped his hands. Very slowly he walked across toward the fop. "Get off yore horse," he said, soft in the throat. "Because I'm goin' to carve it into yore hide, slow and neat lettered, what was really said by that general to keep yore boys from running clear to Charleston. What was really said was, "Look! There is Jackson, standing like a stone wall! Rally behind the Virginians!' " and with a quick hand, he whipped the fop off his horse and he said, "Take off his shirt, boys, while I strop my knife point."

There wasn't a princess in that carriage. There was a very old lady, with a satin bonnet set up top of her ivory hair knot and tied under her ear with a big satin bow. Come to think, maybe she was a princess too. Just grown old. It's always how you believe. She was that old when a person's waking and sleeping runs together all day and all night.

She opened her eyes and said, "Forney Manigault!"

Forney jumped, and everybody looked.

"Yes, ma'am?"

She said, "Forney, whatever are you doing in Manassas? Does your grandmother know you're here?"

Forney's foot shuffled. "Well, Aunt Chastity, as a matter of plain talk, my grandmother sent me."

"She's not sick, is she?"

"No, ma'am. She's right spry still. Right spry."

You could see that Forney was fighting for every minute of time. So Davin helped. He worked the soup-tureen cover out of his cantle pack. He waved Commodus away from Forney's stirrup and undid the gunny bag. He reached inside for Forney's extra drawers with the shattered pieces in it, and the funniest look came on his face, like he had sorghum candy stuck in his throat. Only what he really had was sulphur and molasses all over his hands. Next minute, there was that beautiful Josiah

Wedgwood soup tureen out in the sunlight, without a nick in it, not a crack. Sort of dazed, Davin put the cover on it, and that fine thin china rang in the hot street like a lady's silver table bell.

He walked over and held it out to the old lady. "Davin Ancrum, ma'am. Glad to do a service for Forney's grandma."

"My goodness," Aunt Chastity said. "Cousin Emily's soup bowl. I remember it very well. Cousin Matilda Mesereaux had it from Aunt Augusta Semmes. It was always promised to me."

Forney tugged out his grandmother's letter and handed it up carriage side, and just then the old lady saw Roan standing with one foot on the dandy's neck, the dandy thrashing and flopping under it like an axed rooster. She reached into her reticule for her hand glasses, opened them and held them by the handle in front of her eyes.

"Chesnut," she called, "what are you doing, lying on the ground? ... Forney, that is your cousin Chesnut Haxall from Charleston," and she began to read her letter. After a moment's reading, she said over the top of the letter, "He has come up here to stay with me until they make him a captain or a major or something down in South Carolina.... Chesnut, pick up your hat." After a little bit further reading, she said, "My goodness, Forney; your grandmother says you're in the cavalry."

"Yes, ma'am," Forney grinned. "Looks as if I am."

She said, "But there was a dreadful battle yesterday." She looked over at the rest of the company. "A perfectly dreadful battle. I live out in the country," she explained, "and there were soldiers all over my place all day. The shooting was so close it broke more than two dozen of the windows."

"Sure glad you got away safe, Aunt Chastity."

"Got away?" She put her hand glasses close on Forney. "Got away? I don't know what you mean, Forney. I live at Grammercie. It's my home. I'm in town today because it's my Sewing Day with the Episcopal Mission Board." And then she said, "You weren't in that battle, were you, Forney?"

Forney shuffled foot again. "Well, ma'am," he said, "for a time, I was in a little part of it."

"You weren't hurt, were you, Forney?"

"Well, ma'am, I——"

Roan bowed. "No, ma'am," he said. "Forney weren't hurt at all."

The rest of the summer of 1861 found the Potomac River once more a rough line of demarcation between the difference of opinion. Opposite the city of Washington, the Union forces had troops south of the river but in no consolidated organization that could, in a modern tactical sense, have been called a bridgehead. Alexandria was controlled by these troops. Arlington House, the residence of Colonel Robert Edward Lee, late Corps of Engineers, United States Army, and now an obscure staff officer in Richmond, was used variously as a Union field hospital and a forward echelon headquarters. The Sixty-Ninth, New York, held a shallow bridgehead in Rosslyn, protecting the southern end of the Canal Bridge. This bridge, on the site of which the Key Bridge now stands, brought the canal waters across the Potomac from Georgetown in an open aqueduct so that the canal might serve Alexandria—its mule-drawn boats passing within sight and earshot of the present Pentagon.

A summer war for summer soldiers, after Bull Run, with both armies passing from the offensive—not to the defensive necessarily—but rather to complete apathetic inactivity, with the exception of minor patrol prowling. Confederate cavalry sniffed the outskirts of Alexandria. They came down between Arlington House and Rosslyn and watered their mounts in the Potomac, probably right where the present Memorial Bridge connects the main gates of the Cemetery with the Lincoln Memorial on the Washington side, along the land now occupied by South Post, Fort Meyer.

Across the river they could see the derrick-spidered domeless Capitol, the Washington Monument—flat-topped still, at about one-third of its height to be—and the full raw expanse of the frightened town.

For Washington was frightened, with a victorious armed force to the southward and the whole doubtful but insurgent state of Maryland to the north. The President had sent out an immediate call for additional volunteers and they were pouring in but they were raw. This time, however, they were not coming with the flamboyant bombast of the army that had been soundly trounced at Bull Run. They were coming quietly with a sense of near-disaster in their hearts—and the slow anger that fear instills. They were coming doggedly from the northern farms and cities for it was as if the ghost of Pitcairn was on Lexington Bridge once more, Wellington's Peninsula veterans were marching on Plattsburg, or the last long rifle in the overrun Alamo had ceased to fire.

These men were to be McClellan's mishandled army of the Chickahominy, of Malvern Hill, of Cold Harbor, a hardening breed of men with not so much a personal fight in their hearts as a mass consciousness of which way destiny lay. The United States was the property of their fathers—in their time they would not see it dissipated. Hold the whole farm together and to high hell with hacking off parcels of it to split the ownership!

For Southern arms that summer, the war was won. Bull Run proved it conclusively. Even Congress knew it at last, for Congress had come out to see the battle with its ladies and its picnic lunches and run frantically when the tide turned, leaving a ten-mile trail of broken parasols, top hats, wine bottles, and food hampers.

So what was left? Stay around a while, flushed with the high wine of victory so the Yankees would damn well remember them, and then go home to kiss the girls who had seen them off. Row the Potomac at sundown and have a drink in Willard's just to say you had. Dust up the sentries now and then to keep them awake—but the battle's done and the war's done and that's what we came for. So let's go home.

Not so T. J. Jackson. Nor Beauty Stuart. Nor the rest of the ex-regulars. As they could see through hills in battle, so too they could see through the summer to the painted leaves of fall. In their shoulderblades they could feel the small western actions already probing for control of the Mississippi. In the Atlantic mists they could feel the water envelopment of the Northern navy fending for Cape Fear to blockade the ports. Two fumbling arms as yet, but with their import plain—to embrace both sides of the Confederacy in a wrestler's hug and crush it breathless. So they kept their men to drill schedules, denied them furlough, bent their minds to the cold threat of the massing new armies across the Potomac.

That summer saw the real birth of the greatest army the world has ever seen, the Army of Northern Virginia. Greatest, because it could not be defeated. Shoeless, hungry, short on ammunition always, blanketless in winter, rotten with dysentery, bareheaded to the rains—the Army of Northern Virginia remained upon its feet for four long years. Marched when it was told to march, counter-attacked with the spleen of a hill cat. Won great battles and lost great battles, but always stood to its colors to fight again until it furled those colors in the dignity and awful pride of Appomattox.

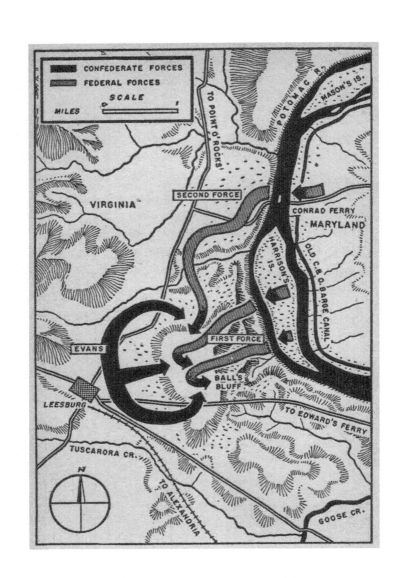

SLAUGHTER AT
BALL'S BLUFF

HADLEY STUART'S GRANDFATHER and his old horse Prince caught up with the Short Mountain Cavalry Company outside of Fairfax Court House a few days after the Bull's Run battle. He was an old man, but he didn't look as old as he was until you looked right close into his eyes. Then you could see the procession of the years going down deep into him like a stone dropped in a blue mountain pool.

"It's like this, sir," he told Roan Catlett. "With Hadley killed, somebody in the Stuart family has to fill in his part. Hadley's ma won't let his brother Ambrose 'list until he turns fifteen. His pa's been dead these six, seven years"—he smiled—"so I reckon that left me."

Roan was slow to smile ever, after Manassas, and with his better than six feet of hill-grown bone and muscle and his leather sunburn he looked much older and meaner than his going on eighteen years should have made him look. It was in Roan's eyes probably that it wouldn't make too much sense having an old man like that in the company. Hadley's grandpappy saw that and he smiled.

"I've got every one of my teeth still anchored solid in m'head, son—and Prince is a good sound horse for all he got old enough to vote this spring." Being called "son" made Roan feel a little homesick, but the thought of a twenty-one-year-old horse made him smile it away fast. "I guess it's all right, sir," he told Hadley's grandfather. "For all of me, you can stay."

"I'm right glad of that, sir, because I told General Lee I'd get his hat and send it to him in Richmond." The old man's eyes twinkled and his head sort of went down toward his left shoulder like he was listening for the laugh that would pick his words up for a joke. But Hadley Stuart was the first boy killed in the company. That day over at Falling Waters when a cannonball hit a tree close enough to General Jackson to plow splinters into his beard. And there wasn't any joke in remembering that. Besides, nobody knew who General Lee was, that early in the war.

Davin Ancrum touched his forehead to the old man. "I'd be right pleased to go get the hat for you, sir, you tell me where he left it. We were powerful fond of Hadley." Forney Manigault frowned. Davin was his cousin, and he knew Davin's way of volunteering to build up credit for a letdown.

Hadley's grandfather snorted. "General Lee didn't really mean get the hat, son! He said it for a joke. When he resigned from the United States Army he left his home and went straight to Richmond. Left everything. Big white house down the Potomac, he and Miz Lee had. Called it Arlington House. Remember it long ago. Pillars in front and a portrait of George Washington in the parlor. Overlooks a slope to the river. But the Yankees took it over right away as a headquarters; so that does for the hat. But it was a right special hat, I reckon. You know how some men are? Placing great store in certain hats? When he gave me my letter in Richmond and I thanked him, he laughed and said, 'I left my hat up there on the Potomac, where you're going, sir. If you can get it back for me, that'll return the slight courtesy I've been able to do you.'" The old man's eyes got sort of wistful. "Joke or not, I'd sure like to get that hat, to return General Lee's courtesy to me. But it's impossible, so I reckon we'll just forget it.... Whoa-up, Prince! Stand still, y'hear?"—which wasn't necessary because the old horse was sound asleep where he stood, and had been all the time.

Now the order in the company from Roan was to go light on Hadley's grandpappy, and on that old black horse, Prince.

Let him work as hard as he wanted, only damn well see that the heavy work was done before he got to it, and damn well don't let him know it was planned that way.

It wasn't any chore to do that, for Mr. Stuart was likable. He could cook like a sailor cooks—take anything for a base, add anything you had to offer, and come up with real tasty potluck. He could tell time by the stars, give him a moment to look—and never off only a few minutes, and maybe at that it was the clock you checked by that was off, not him. He'd been a sailor and been all over the world. It was in his walk somewhat and the way he'd ask, "Smoking lamp lit?" when he wanted a pipe on night patrol. But he didn't offer talk. Not like most oldsters, cankering the spleen in you, telling how it was in their day.

Day patrols'd shove over wide, southeast, and water their horses right in the Potomac River with the whole mud-flat Washington City right across, to see it all. Night patrols'd push around close to the head of the Aqueduct Bridge, listening to those New York Irishmen jasperooing each other in their camp. Sixty-ninth Regiment it was, guarding the bridge, and come sundown the whisky'd flow red. Their Colonel Corcoran had got himself captured in the battle and sent to Richmond—and he was the only one they'd ever kept order for. So all bets were off until he got exchanged.

One night on point, dismounted, Forney and Davin got in close enough listening, to fall over one of those New York boys sleeping whisky deep. Fall didn't even blink him, but it tinkled his bottle, so they took it off him in the name of Jeff Davis and went on around and down to the riverbank to look the situation over.

"Right good bourbon," Davin said.

"Store bought. Thin," Forney said.

Davin pointed across river. "Couple of boys in Jeb Stuart's regiment tell me they went right into Washington one night and bought drinks at Kirkwood's Hotel on Twelfth Street."

"How?" Forney turned his head sharp.

"Boat," Davin said.

"In uniform they'd 'a' been caught. Out of uniform ain't honest." That's the Manigault family for you always.

"What uniform?" Davin reached for the bottle back. "Both of us got the fundamental clothes on we wore at home. Shirts and pants. Take off the sabers and hats, and we're just country boys in for marketing."

"What boat?" Forney grunted.

"Right down there," Davin pointed. "With everybody saying the war's over, I'd sure hate to miss seeing Washington before I go back to school—especially the Capitol where my daddy used to orate." Mighty fine orator, Senator Ancrum. Powerful chest and throat.

The boat didn't leak too badly and the next thing Forney knew, Davin was paddling it right down the middle of the Potomac. Only thing Forney could think was that he wasn't going to let his cousin go alone, even if it wasn't what a Manigault would do, left on his own to decide.

Wind was off the city and the place smelled worse than Manassas battlefield. Sour sick. Old swamp they built the town on—with a stench of fudged sewage simmering in the damp heat to make the fish-rot river flats a relief until their boat got opposite that stone shaft they were going to finish someday in memory of George Washington. The Yankee Army had its slaughterhouse there and the fetid leavings covered half a rotting green acre, four feet deep.

By that time the bottle was done. Besides, the moon broke out from the clouds and they could see the Capitol straight down the sludge canal, all cobwebbed with derricks and scaffolds, and no dome on it yet, which was what they'd come to see. Where Senator Ancrum orated. On top of all, three or four sentries were shooting at them from the riverbank now, so Davin turned the boat and headed back.

"Looka there, Forney!" he said. "There's that general's house where he left his hat!"

And sure enough, up the slope in the trees in the moonlight there was a big house with white pillars like old Mr. Stuart had said.

Forney said, "Let's not stop, boy! Them bullets are getting close to hitting, we take a deep breath to make ourselves a mite wider!"

"Sure was good bourbon," Davin grinned.

They made back to below Anolostan Island, beached the boat and went on back to where they'd left the patrol with the horses. Only thing was Roan was there, come down to inspect, and he smelled the liquor on them. Going to take the hide off them in quick long-arm jerks, not for touching the stuff on duty but for touching it, that's all—when old Mr. Lovatt Stuart said, "Sergeant, I gave them a half issue of my own medicinal rum apiece," and he patted his saddle bag. "Against the malaria. Medicine. Pure medicine. They were coming down, else."

He was like that, the old man. Sharp as a whistle for the right thought and word in trouble. Like an old soldier.

When everybody knew finally that Beauregard wasn't going to take Washington, he said, "I'm sort of glad. It got taken once by the British. Wasn't pretty. Army ran away at Bladensburg. Captain Barney's sailors came up from the mosquito fleet, running with cannons on their shoulders. Tried to save it, but Barney got wounded and it was all over. British burned the Printing Office and the Treasury and the President's Palace. President Jim Madison ran away to Maryland. Dignity bled clean out of the country for a while. Wasn't pretty." He shook his head slowly. "This yere's a family fight. Blood feuding, but we're all Americans, don't forget. So let's fight each other like men; let's not get to burning out each other's houses, like banditti." He smiled. "I talk too much."

When Col. Jeb Stuart first saw old Mr. Stuart, he looked twice, quick, and kneed over to him. "I don't place your name, sir? You've just joined?" It wasn't for any reason at first, except that Colonel Jeb had to get names. Knew all names of his three hundred men. Called them plain, day or night. Captains to cooks.

"Lovatt Stuart, sir." Then he saw the colonel's eye cloud just a shade at the sight of how old he was and how old Prince was, sleeping sound there on formation under him. Sound, to horse snores. The fire kindled deep to pride in the old man's own eyes. "Total age of horse and man," he said, "one hundred years." And that was right. He was seventy-nine and Prince was twenty-one, like it or leave it.

Colonel Stuart was only twenty-eight years old that year, and he didn't like it. You could see that. A cavalryman's got hard work to do, and there're two ways it can't be done. One is to try to be a hero, so the others always have to get you out of show-off trouble; and the other is always to need help the other way, from lack of strength or spirit, horse or man. Either way takes it from the files to right and left and weakens the command. That was in Jeb Stuart's mind, and you could almost see fear in the old man's eyes when he saw it there. If he got to be sent away before Ambrose reached fifteen, it would let the whole family down.

"I have a letter," he said, "from General Robert Edward Lee, sir. I didn't aim to show it"—he pulled it out of pocket and held it in hand—"but if it's going to be going home or not——I'd sure like to stay for just one battle."

Colonel Jeb looked quick at Roan Catlett with the question.

Roan snapped his hand up, flicking his hat brim. "Pulls his freight, sir," Roan said. "Lifts his weight. Shore sorry to have to lose him, sir."

"Proud to have you with us, sir." Colonel Jeb bowed slightly. "The letter won't be necessary as long as Sergeant Catlett vouches for you. Unless it's to me personally."

"It's to 'Whom-it-may-concern,' sir. Thank you, sir," and the old man put the letter back in. Later he said to Roan, "Thank you kindly, sergeant—if you weren't lying?" and Roan couldn't quite meet his eye. He just said, "No man lies to Colonel Stuart twice," and the meaning was plain between them.

"I understand," the old man said. "You won't regret it, sir."

The summer wore along. The war was over. All the hotheads were yelling for discharges or furlough to go home and tell how they won it. But Gen. "Stonewall" Jackson wasn't going home, so he didn't let his men go. Nor was Colonel Jeb, so his regiment stayed too. Drilling.

After McDowell, the Yankees got a fellow named McClellan in command and along toward the end of September the war wasn't over at all. Word got around that there was a sizable Yankee force camped between Conrad's and Edward's Ferries near Harrison's Island on the Upper Potomac. Our left, under Gen. "Shanks" Evans, who had the riflemen at Bull's Run, was secured on Leesburg, but they were shy on cavalry scouts, so early in October the Short Mountain Company, being Shenandoah boys, got ordered up under this Evans to help scout for the Mississippi infantry—13th, 17th and 18th regiments.

It was in the air that something was going to rip. The cork was still in the bottle on Sunday morning, the twentieth, but you could feel it sizzing to pop. The company rode into Drainesville just at first light and broke into prowl points of four to scout the river line. Roan, old Mr. Stuart, Davin and Forney took the right-hand east flank, and coming up on Ball's Bluff, dismounted, and began to look-see Harrison's Island opposite and the far shore.

Suddenly the old man pointed. "Boats," he said. "Flatboats from the Chesapeake Canal. Soldiers in 'em."

"Don't make sense," Davin shook his head. "This side the bluff is too steep to climb up to here. Must be a hundred, hundred fifty feet straight up almost from the water to where we are. Why boat over to the island, opposite here? It don't make sense."

"It made sense when Wolfe did it at Quebec," Mr. Stuart whispered. "A fellow once said, 'Never say a cliff's inaccessible; just say difficult for horse artillery.'"

Roan chewed grass. "Like this way, you think, sir? Sneak over here and up the bluff face because we wouldn't think they could? Start the fight up-river a piece and fall on our flank from here?"

"It could be," the old man nodded.

"Cripes," Roan snorted. "It's your idea, sir; you ride dispatch in and take the word to General Evans. Fast."

You'd never forget that picture of Mr. Stuart against the autumn sky. When he crawled back to Prince, the old horse was asleep as usual, but he woke up and flared his nostrils and pranced a little bit to show he wasn't. Mr. Stuart threw a leg over and straight in the saddle, raised his hand with his hat in it to Roan and the others. Prince seemed to feel something, too, for he ups with his fore-hoofs and to hell with his rheumatism. The cavalier, the man on horseback, the spirit of the battle that only one sculptor in a thousand can see in the cold stone he carves his statue from. "Total age of horse and man, one hundred years."

Well, that's the way it was, you'll read in cold history print. Two forces. One to cross between Edward's Ferry and Conrad's. The other from Harrison's Island and up the cliff, to catch Shanks Evans between and run him out of Leesburg. Only Shanks wasn't there. Which saved trouble, because the Yankees didn't get there either. Where they did get the next day was each halfway, when the cork popped. The force that climbed Ball's Bluff was mostly Massachusetts people. General Evans let 'em move down almost to Leesburg before he let go. They must have been the feint, because they fell back right away, leaving only one man dead. But the sound of the battle brought the other force down to help, and shortly after noon Evans had them pinned cold, on three sides, to the top of Ball's Bluff. That was no Bull's Run. It was stand and deliver and lash it out for blood. New Yorkers now with the Massachusetts men—40th Regiment by the belt plates on the dead—and they said the 1st California Regiment was somewhere in it, too—mostly Pennsylvanians and elsewhere, however, which is what they say Californians are.

Just before twilight, old Mr. Stuart found the company again, where it was being held off, shelter of the woods, for when the cavalry mop-up would begin.

"I didn't stay away, sergeant," he told Roan. "I was kept by General Evans for dispatch and guiding."

"That's all right," Roan nodded, his eyes keen to the fight across the way. "I figured so." But what he was really figuring was when the charge order came, there'd be the old man with him on his old horse, Prince, and it getting toward dark and the bluff edge steep and all. The way a man thinks who's got twenty men to think for. And he sure didn't want to charge old Mr. Stuart and that twenty-one-year-old horse, Prince. He sure as hell-fire didn't. Across the bluff top, the gun smoke was blue in the twilight, hanging like autumn mist, gashed with red as the firing got hotter.

Where the company waited there was a mask of oaks, and the leaves now and then would drift down from long shots high above. It was coming up on cavalry time now, fast, for the Massachusetts men and the New Yorkers were slowly backing to the cliff top. Fascinating to watch. Like a boat drifting toward the open lip of a waterfall. In a moment the word would come galloping in the twisted mouth of one of General Evans' staff: "Cavalry to clear the field! Draw ... sabers!" and Roan sure enough didn't want to charge Mr. Stuart and that old horse, Prince.

It was in his eyes of course. Mr. Stuart saw it, and a man can't keep begging and hold his pride forever. "The poet Homer once said"—the old man's voice was soft—"that 'that man is happy who has sons and whose sons have sons, and who himself is permitted to die upon the field of battle.' " But before Roan could say, "How's that, sir?" there was a sound like a boot sucking mud and Prince threw up his head in awful surprise, slewed around like his hind hoofs had slipped on slick, and started to go down slowly all over. Mr. Stuart was off and at his mount's head before the old horse was quite down. They just sort of looked at each other—just looked—and Prince made a noise in his throat, when the pink foam bubbled through his nostrils, that you would have sworn was a laugh at some old and homely joke they had between them. "And I reckon that goes for horses too." The old man looked up at Roan. "Satisfy your function in life, and be able to recapture a figment of youth again at the very end." He eased Prince's girth and drew the saddle off his dead horse. "Made Prince feel mighty good, being with the younger horses."

Then they all saw the word coming; saw the officer galloping in, his hat gone and the wind tangled in his hair; saw his face twist in a shout drowned by the firing.

Roan turned taut to the boys. "Dismount and tighten girths! … Mr. Stuart," he said, "we'll see you later."

It wasn't a battle from that time on; it was slaughter. The poor devils taken on three sides against the bluff top went over it. Some tried to scale down. More got pushed. There were knives in it and clubbed rifles, with the autumn-darkness sea blue to full black, and the cliffside screaming with lost souls, to the water's edge.

Some tried to swim. Some tried to get off in the boats. By then the company was afoot, horses with the holders on top, fighting down side by side the Mississippi infantry. One boat got off and sank, then another, and another.

It was Davin Ancrum who found Mr. Stuart. He hadn't gone to the stragglers' line at all; he'd made for the cliff top and climbed down east of the fight, worked his way to twenty feet above the river, where the boats were beached, and crouched there, deliberately shooting holes in the bottoms of them with his Sharps carbine and his hand gun. Smashing the rudders and riddling the planks. Maybe he didn't win the battle, but he sure fixed it so precious few Yankees got back across the river to tell how they lost it.

Had to carry the old man up, he was that exhausted. He couldn't talk. It had just run his strength out, doing that. The last of it. All he had left. But it was worse than that. He wanted it to be that way. With his old horse, Prince, shot dead under him, the whole adventure was closing up. The accounts totted. He'd had his battle and that's all there was. Davin was crying—not really; just the tears flooding his eyes. "We'll get you another horse, sir," kneeling beside him in the firelight, begging up to Roan Catlett with his eyes, while Forney put more blankets to keep the old man warm. Roan shook his head. Davin pulled him aside. "But don't let him die, Roan," he begged. "He just lies there smiling. You've got to do something, Roan."

It was awful watching that faded smile touched across that old white face like a benediction. From all the years back it came through, like evening sun after a storm. Davin shook his head again. "And he didn't even get to get that general's hat he talked about!"

John Lasater came up with Prince's saddle where the old man had left it on the cliff top. They touched his lips with his own rum and he went to sleep then. Old sleep, soft breathed. Davin held the bottle. Roan just walked away.

Forney said, "Don't take on so, Davin. He had sons and grandsons—and Ball's Bluff was sure a field of battle while it lasted," and he rolled into his own blanket.

"I'm going to get that hat for him," Davin said fiercely, standing there in the firelight with the flame writhing on his face and the rum bottle in his hand. Fighting does fey things to the mind. It takes the real, and shadows it in fantasy, while fantasy will stay in it for years, crouching beyond the edge of memory. Davin was there for a moment to his cousin Forney, with the crimson yellow fire ribbons lacing across his face and that bottle of rum uncorked in hand. The next minute the fire was gone in the flaked white ash of dawn, but Davin was still there, this time with the hat in his hand, holding it out in white anger, sobbing, "You let him die, damn you! You let him die!"

With Davin, the time between was almost as fast, for he saw himself go and get back, before he even started. That was the rum, sloshed down raw on battle shock. He saw himself sneak to the *piquet* line and rope out his mount, onsaddle and lead to the road. Mount and start. Passing sentries at the gallop, shouting, "Dispatch for Colonel Jeb Stuart!" Walking between, to save his mount. Circling Centerville to avoid question and riding wide of Fairfax under the full arch of deep night. There were gaps in it which was the rum, too, for old Mr. Stuart carried powerful seagoing medicine. But it was awfully clear being close in the bushes to that big white house with the six pillars looking down the broad grass sward to the Potomac. Awfully clear in Davin's mind that it had to be that General Lee's house because the Yankees were sure enough using it for some kind of a headquarters. There were the slow sounds of sentries' feet on the gravel drive in back and, in what light there was, the glint of bayonets on their muskets. What would make it sure was the picture of George Washington in the parlor.

Davin went over the lawn slowly, on his belly, the way it was taught in drill, clinging to shadows tight with his shirt buttons. Close to the wall, he inched along, figuring to find a window into the cellar that he could force with his spring knife, and climb up into the house from below.

His mind was on George Washington's picture now, because that was the next step to take to be sure he was in the right place. When he got into the cellar, he took his boots off and hung them around his neck before he groped in the darkness for stairs up. But when he got up, there wasn't much need, for the carpets were thick underfoot. Only thing was, you had to be mighty careful opening doors, for they were big doors, swollen in their frames with the night damp. There were people, too, in the back, the way people are at night when the hours are working down the slope toward morning. A spurred boot slipping off a desk top. The smell of stale coffee, reheated, and tobacco smoke stenching damp and thin and bitter. Soldiers. Orderlies and staff officers of whatever headquarters it was made into. There was yellow lamp-light splashed down some of the halls. This General Lee must have been a very wealthy man for a house this size and this richly furnished. Silk-covered chairs and sofas. Pictures, and suddenly one of those pictures was George Washington in the distant smear of lamplight, on his gray horse with his sword pointing straight out at Davin Ancrum.

That made him sure of the house, and a great warmth of accomplishment came over him. He felt good inside and big and powerful in his muscles. But time wasn't standing still. So he inched out into the great hall and started to work down side-ways, close to the wall, watching the sweep of stairs above and the light splash of the headquarters office and holding his breath. Right beside the door, he saw the hat. There were half a dozen blue Yankee kepis on the chest top beside it, so it was easy to tell General Lee's. Very carefully he reached out his hand, crouching to get his arm to go far enough, and his fingers closed over the stiff brim. He drew it to him and worked back up the hall, hold-ing it tight to his stifled chest.

It seemed to take him hours longer to get out of the house, down cellar, out the forced window and across the lawns on his belly. When he was clear, he ran to make up time—ran all the way to where he'd left his boat. Climbed up the slope to where he'd left his horse and started the long way back to the company bivouac.

When Forney opened his eyes, there Davin stood, with the hat held out, cursing him soft in his teeth, "You let him die, damn you! You let him die!"

Roan was kneeling beside old Mr. Stuart chafing his hands and trying to poke up the fire between, and there was a young fellow there with Roan, his blanket roll at his feet, with a squirrel rifle laid overtop and his horse still saddled just beyond.

"Shut up!" Roan said. "He's not dead."

Davin yelled, "I got the hat for him—to send to his friend in Richmond! The general who gave him the letter!"

Forney woke up and saw Davin there with the hat the way he'd been there with the rum bottle just a minute before, it seemed like.

"This yere's Ambrose Stuart," Roan said. "Hadley's brother. He just turned fifteen. Been riding to jine us .... Shut up, Davin!"

That was when old Mr. Stuart opened his eyes. "Hello, Ambrose," he said.

Ambrose said, "Yore to go straight home, grandfer." He turned to Davin and Forney and Roan. "He's real old," he said softly. "He fought down there at Bladensburg in eighteen fourteen with Barney. A midshipman, he was. On the Hamilton when she sank the British frigate Penelope off Montauk. Down at Veracruz last war, against the Mexicans."

"Keep quiet, Ambrose," the old man said. "You talk too much."

And Davin said, "Here's the hat, sir. I got it for you—for your friend, General Lee."

Old Mr. Stuart looked up at Davin as if he didn't rightly understand. "What would General Lee do with a hat like that, son?"

"Well, sir, I don't rightly know about what he'd do with it. I didn't figure that. Just that you wanted his hat to send to him. So I got it for you, sir."

"Where? Where'd you get it?"

"From his house. Where the Yankee soldiers had all their hats. The big white house with the six pillars that overlooks down to the Potomac."

Old Mr. Stuart pushed up in his blankets and reached out a hand. He took the hat and stared at it for a minute. "By Jeremy," he said, "I ain't agoin' home! ... Son," he said to Davin, "you mistook the house! You got the wrong side of the river! ... Sergeant," he said, "can I stay if I get another horse?" and he was up on his feet then. "Look at the name in that hat," he shouted, "and try to pry me loose from this man's army, and I'll really show my letter!"

Roan looked in the hat and he looked at Davin, and he walked slow across and smelled his breath.

"You've been drinkin', Davin," he said, "and this time I'm goin' to whip you for it. Put up yore hands!"

The hat rolled over to Forney. He looked at the name. Those Manigaults are the most honest people in the whole world. He said to Ambrose, "How in the hell are we going to get this hat he stole—back to Mr. Lincoln?"

Midway that first summer of the war it became evident to Richmond that the massing of Union troops in the vicinity of Chambersburg, Pennsylvania, as well as at Washington, constituted two separate capabilities of attack when the new armies were ready to march. One capability was a straight drive south on the Confederate capital. The other was a drive through the lush granary of the Shenandoah Valley to envelop Richmond from the rear.

Whereas Jackson had made a name for himself, of sorts, at Bull Run, as a combat general officer, he was not yet immortal. It was the Stonewall Brigade at that time rather than he himself as Stonewall Jackson, and among the galaxy of bright stars at Bull Run, he was still a middle-ranking Brigadier. He was, however, known by higher authority as a most competent officer for the training of new troops. The performance of his brigade at Bull Run was credited to the fact that in a matter of weeks he had trained them from raw separate units into a coordinated command that could perform well in combat.

So he was relieved of his brigade at Centreville and sent, without troops, to Winchester with the mission of organizing the new militia levées into a Valley Army for the defense of the Shenandoah. Through the fall and winter he did his job well for two anachronistic reasons. The one was that he gradually acquired as cavalry the highly individualistic and poorly disciplined force of Turner Ashby. Ashby was not a professional soldier, nor had he any intention of aping one in manner or method; but he could screen for Jackson, he could get information and he would fight for it viciously, if need be.

The other reason was that at Christmas time Jackson requested and got his old First Brigade as a nucleus, an example of training, a veteran corps around which he could mold his new army to the First Brigade's template of performance.

Turner Ashby's war was personal. He was the finest horseman in Virginia at the time and he could draw unto himself all the hotspurs who loved a horse, a jug, and a girl's smile. He could lead them too, as long as they were in units small enough for him to control personally and visually. But he had no facility at decentralization of command, nor had the command itself been trained by him in any concept of coordinated action. Again, Virginia to Ashby meant his home at Rose Hill and the adjacent Valley he had hunted in. It meant his brother who had been killed early and on whose grave Turner had sworn a private and awful vengeance. Beyond that, he had no strategic concepts. Yet he served Jackson well, riding circuit eternally on the broad arc of the river that cut across the northern entrance to the Valley. Scouting the Union preparations for advance, even to going himself into their camps in disguise when necessary. It is inconceivable that any man of Ashby's command needed a map or a compass. They were native sons, operating on their own terrain, knowing the trails and bypaths since boyhood, out on their own good horses, with their own good rifles, in defense of their own splendid Valley with a pride and arrogance that lies deep in the Shenandoah breed.

Roan Catlett, when his company joined Ashby, was of an age when boys are crystallized into soldiers, if soldiering lies in their hearts. Had Stuart kept him in his command he would have been subjected to the full treatment of cavalry discipline and been a better man. With Ashby he was not. Roan admired Ashby for his incisive daring and worked for him well, but he could not love him. It was like a gay expensive school in which the boys know they are wasting their father's hopes and substance, and a discomfort sits upon the better minds. For Roan, Ashby never quite came off. Jackson and J. E. B. Stuart were the breed any soldier could love. They always accomplished their missions to the letter of their orders, but, within that military necessity of the regular, they gave *paramount consideration to their men. Ashby could not, for the very concept of it was left out of him. He was an individualist, so were his men. What they did, they did in small units with a sort of temporary mass enthusiasm for the job in hand. Thereafter, it was taken for granted they could look out for themselves. But men cannot, in war, for there is nothing more helpless than an individual in mass, when his commanding officer fails to realize that the basic component of men is man.*

The winter wore on into spring, the wet and frost-shot spring of '62. The bright victory of Manassas was a blade long tarnished now by time. The Union odds to the northward had slowly become overwhelming both in numbers and equipment when totted man for man and gun for gun against Jackson's small force.

In Washington, McClellan commanded; under him, McDowell. Little Mac, the white-haired boy of the Union forces. The small western actions for the control of the Mississippi had begun to assume the outward and visible signs of a rolling campaign. The Navy was closing the Atlantic ports of the Confederacy. What Stuart and Jackson had seen in the summertime was now written plain for all men to see. And the picture was not pleasant.

Alone to the northward stood Virginia, offering the terrain and most of the manpower against the full brunt of the spring attacks. Offering her farms to be overrun, her homes to be lost. Women to be stricken blind in their souls when their loves were killed in the field. Children, with their hearts to be broken in tiny pieces.

But against that time of travail, a tall and bearded man began to assume his immortal stature. Thomas Jonathan Jackson, one-time lieutenant of guns at Chapultepec, one-time schoolteacher at Lexington, all-time wrestler with his literal, living God. A close student of Napoleon for over fifteen years. Close friend to no man, for he was too hard to know. Kindly to all men in his thinking, even when duty lashed him to contained but frightful anger—as it did once against Ashby. But a soldier of soldiers, for in addition to his pastmastery of combined arms tactics he had the broader strategical vision that completes the military cycle.

The ending of one military operation to Jackson was the immediate and uninterrupted beginning of the next. No battle was justified unless it wove itself deftly into the whole fabric of the war. Jackson, therefore, became the empiric father of the modern American military doctrine. That is why he is great in history. One knows it now, in cold reason.

But in the spring of '62 one knew only what was in men's hearts when they saw him great-coated by the roadside. "Stonewall Jackson—for the Valley!"

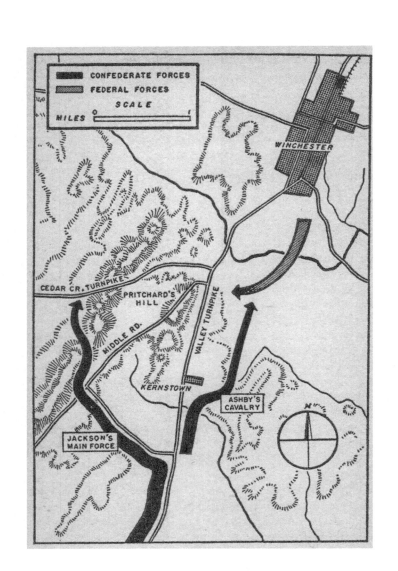

WHY STONEWALL
JACKSON GOT LICKED
AT KERNSTOWN

I T WAS WELL AFTER NOON when Roan Catlett's horse was hit. Stretched full to clear a stone wall north of Stephenson's, getting away from a close-in scout on the Yankee west flank. Roan heard the bullet strike, like tobacco spit hitting loose board. Felt Jason flicker at the top of the jump, like breaking a taut silk thread. Forney Manigault was ahead of him, left, with Davin Ancrum intervaled out to the right and Colonel Ashby thundering along behind at the gallop.

Turner Ashby pulled up his own milk-white on the other side of the ridge line, spun her on her heels with the wind in his black beard and flung off. "Your mount's hit, Catlett. Let's look." There were frost crusts along the hollows and the cold spleen of March was bitter in the air. Roan was off, holding Jason's head, looking at his eyes close for pain.

Turner Ashby put a hand to Jason's off flank; touched beside the entering wound with a gentle gloved finger. Walked around quickly to the near side. Bent close, his dark, fine-planed face clenched at the eyes. Two weeping bullet rips, you could cover with a two-bit piece each. One each side where it had gone clean through. Turner Ashby looked quick into Roan's desperate question.

"Blanket him and walk him slow. If you can get him to Doc Tatly in Winchester he may have a chance. The doc performs miracles with hosses, keep him drunk enough. Sorry, Catlett. Fine animal.... Manigault!" He unbuckled his near saddle bag and drew out the roll of newspapers. Baltimore, Washington, Philadelphia and New York papers picked up each scout, from roadside and old bivouacs where the Yankees dropped them after reading. Tom, muddy or what—the order was "Get their newspapers." "Take these papers in to General Jackson's headquarters and tell 'em the Yankee advance guard will be about four miles from Winchester come nightfall. Last I knew, Jackson's headquarters was at Taylor's Hotel in Winchester. That's all." Colonel Ashby mounted his milk-white. "Rejoin when you can. We'll be somewhere." And he was gone in the mists like nothing so much as the quick flash of a deer's brush in white birch. Turner Ashby of Rose Hill. God rest his gallant soul.

The three troopers climbed wearily up through the scrub oak toward the Unger's Store Road, leading their mounts. Three old men, not yet twenty summers grown, but with no laughter left in them. Last November end to this March beginning had killed their laughter. Screening the hundred-mile arc of the Potomac across the mouth of the Shenandoah Valley against General Banks' thirty-eight-thousand-man Yankee power play had sapped their youth. November to March, with the Southern ports on the Atlantic falling one by one to the Northern fleet; with the armies of the West yielding up the Mississippi, battle by battle, until Virginia alone was the only saber pointing sharp at the bastions of the North. Virginia, hell; only Jackson, for east of the Blue Ridge the word now was that last summer's victorious Manassas army was falling back to the Rapidan under heavy pressure. And that left Stonewall Jackson alone, out on a limb, pinched in the Shenandoah Valley, outnumbered, outgunned, with the whole right wing of McClellan's quarter-million-man new army pouring down on him like spring rains swollen in the rivers. That will kill youth and laughter.

Top of the rise, Forney Manigault mounted stiffly with the newspapers strapped to his pommel roll. His chapped lips rasped open, blood-beaded, to speak. But there were no words. He kneed his mount and took off across the flat for the Unger's Store Road. Roan and Davin could see him get smaller and smaller, until he lifted over the rail fence a couple of miles west—a black bug galloping toward Winchester.

Davin Ancrum, racked with chill, pulled himself slowly up onto his own saddle. His jacket sleeve was caked white with nose run, his reddened eyes rheumed his frost-burned cheekbones.

"Lean down," Roan said, and he put a dirt-crusted hand up to behind Davin's ear. "You got fever, Davin. Pull loose yore blanket and wrap in it."

Davin said, "No! Let be."

They walked, Roan leading both horses, Davin sitting his. Slow, with the tarnished yellow sun smoking cold to slide behind Little North Mountain in another two hours.

You get so tired in war. Sleep can't lift it, for it builds up slow inside, and solidifies like old age, and there is only wisdom left, with less and less strength to carry it. Roan knew his horse was going to die. Knew he'd have to shoot him soon. First sure-enough horse Roan ever had. Watched him swell slow in golden Dolly's belly the long spring and summer he was just past his own thirteenth birthday. Watched Dolly foal by lantern light. "Stallion, Roan, and all yours. That's the blood of Timoleon you see in the colt's eyes. He's a gentleman, Roan. Treat him like one."

Dying on his feet now on the Unger's Store Road to Winchester, the way Jackson's tiny army would die in its next battle—and the whole Southern cause with it. Defeat and desperation galled the soul of Roan Catlett and his blood was rancid in his veins.

Coming down into Winchester, he could see the Pioneers trenching across the Valley Pike. Standing gaunt in the twilight against the distant Massanutton peaks, to ease their backs.

"What's the word, scout?" and a jerked chin to the north, with the question hard in the eye. Valley men, asking of the Valley. A personal war this second spring. Every man jack for his own family now, with the deed to his land in the rifle in his hands, and the early-spring working of it in his ditching shovel.

"They're comin'," Roan said. "Tomorrow. Next day."

The diggers looked north again and spat and gripped their shovels once more. "Let 'em come, scout." Thirty-eight thousand against forty-five hundred. "Let 'em come, scout"—and you could cry if there were any tears left.

It was full dark now and the evening wind of March was knife-sharp under the bare branches arched above the Winchester streets, worrying, like old people's distant voices. There were heel taps in the darkness on the brick-paved walks far ahead, as if they scurried from Roan and Davin to leave them deeper in their misery.

Then right beside where they passed, from the deeper dark of a tree shadow, Forney Manigault's sore throat rasp, "Roan! Ya'll took long enough. Turn in yere."

Roan had both bridles—Jason's and Davin's. He turned in through the shadow sentinels of high gateposts to fine gravel underfoot that splashed like brook water, with Forney moving to walk beside him. "I found this yere Doc Tatly for yore hoss Jason, and a bed for the night for Davin to rest in good. And hot suppuh for us all."

As he said it a stable door opened and splashed warm yellow light into the cold dark above them, and there was a young girl standing. Proud; like a young empress almost, out of a storybook. Full-skirted and slender, facing into the night with no fear of what it held below her. Her face shrouded in shadow, but beauty in it full.

Davin jerked his head up and saw the girl. He leaned full to his mount's neck to steady with both hands as he disengaged his off stirrup and slid heavily to the ground, shaking miserably with chill, his hat in both hands. "Davin—Ancrum, ma'am."

With one hand to Davin to steady him, Roan bowed. "Roan Catlett," he said. "The Short Mountain Cavalry Comp'ny, ma'am. Brigaded now with Colonel Turner Ashby."

"Yes." Her voice was thin in the cold night air. "This is the home of Colonel Lentaigne. He is away, but you are most welcome. I am his daughter, Molly Lentaigne." There was cool, studied dignity in the way she said it. A young gentlewoman offering the hospitality of her father's home to strangers. And then, because it sounded stilted to her when it was finally spoken, she warmed it with quiet eagerness. "My brother is Brace Lentaigne. He's with Colonel Ashby too. You haven't seem him lately, have you?"

Roan said, "I regret I don't know yore brother, Miss Molly."

She moved her head sharply, almost as if she felt offense. "Just lead the horses up the ramp," she said; "then we'll get the sick man into bed."

She stepped into darkness to push the stable door wider.

Inside, there was a little fat man in baggy black pants and a dirty gray claw-hammer coat dragged low to his hips each side, as if he had chimney bricks in his pockets.

"Tatly, the hoss doctuh," he said. "At yore service. Which un's the hurt hoss?" Then he walked slow over to Jason and took his jaw gently in hand. "You, hunh? What yo' mean gettin' yoreself shot by a damyankee? Big hoss like you? Ought to know bettah. Six year old," he said. "Timoleon blood by yore line too. Stand still while I look," and he lifted off the blanket.

"You know this hoss, sir?" Roan asked.

"Know all Valley hosses," doc spat. "Oncet I look at un. Good thing I do too. Because I think foh um and jolly um, and they know I do."

"Name's Jason," Roan told him.

"Hold the lantern," doc told him, but as he said it, the light of the lantern flooded up toward them, and through it Roan saw a twelve-year-old girl, holding it high. He smiled at her and winked in friendliness. She raised a finger to her lips and moved her head slightly toward Davin, sunk down in the straw, his back against the barn wall behind.

"Your friend's got measles," the girl whispered. "Spots all over his face. But it'll shame him to have a child's disease, being a trooper of Colonel Ashby's"—she shook her head—"so we won't tell him, shall we? Just pretend—fever?"

Roan stared at her. "Measles are catching," he grunted. "We'll have to tell yore sister. It won't be right for us to stay yere now."

"We can't tell my sister," the little girl said. "On account of the baby. But it won't matter if she doesn't know. We'll put him in the downstairs bedroom I had last year when I had measles. That'll be far enough away. And there is a big bottle of turpentine and opium that was left after I got well."

"Yore sister's married?"

"You have to be married to have a baby, silly. Only she hasn't had it yet. Another day or two, they think."

"You mean the young lady——" Roan turned and looked out into the black beyond the open stable door. "You mean Miss Molly?"

The girl stared at him as if he had suddenly gone out of his reason.

"You're making fun of me," she told Roan quietly, "because I let my hems out," and there was a bright glint in her wide eyes as an angry tear glaze filmed them. "*I'm* Molly Lentaigne."

Roan swallowed hard, looked again toward the open door and back at the little girl. "You stood so tall, there on the ramp above—with no light on yore face, and so dignified that I thought you were"—he smiled—"I thought you were a mite older—than you are, Miss Molly." And he bowed, and the way he said it this time was not mocking, not just fun with a child. It was honest respect, and she knew it.

She dropped her full curtsy to him, with color in her cheeks and her eyes lowered, and for just a moment the seven years between them were seven years on ahead. Not now, but on ahead where youth always lives, and where Roan had stopped living ever again from too much war. Just for a second, she wasn't twelve; she was nineteen. And just for a second, his nineteen was twenty-six, and a strange embarrassment caught him full, for the line between girl and woman can be a very thin one at times.

Jason began to go down between them. Went down like an old dog to sleep in the straw. Drew himself together in a half turn as if to mat grass; curved in on himself very slowly to bring the whole of him close to his hurting, let his knees buckle and sank down with a soft noise in his nostrils and a long, tired stretch of his neck.

"Sure, sure." Old Tatly knelt beside him, his hand on his cheek. "You take it easy now, Jason hoss. Yo're among friends, y'ole fool!"

Roan hunkered down and laid his hand soft to Jason's neck, and at the touch it was his father's stable six years before, with golden Dolly birthwet in the lantern light, with little Jason born all new again with his great wobbly legs struggling to stand. Through the distortion of his own filmed eyes, Roan looked hard at old Tatly.

"Colonel Ashby told me you could do miracles, suh. If you can't, with this hoss, you tell me in time, y'hear? If he has to be— shot"—Roan fisted his chest hard so the blow echoed like a drum thump—"I'll shoot him. Nobody else." He stood up quickly to steady himself, and in that moment when he desperately needed it, the little girl put her hand in his. "He'll be all right, Mr. Catlett," she said. "You'll see."

They took Davin up the gravel drive to the house. Roan sponge-bathed him and got him to bed. Then, in some way that

Roan didn't quite understand, or try to, he was walking toward Taylor's Hotel with the little girl, his saber rattling like peddler's pots, his spurs singing on brick. Things happen like that when you're dog-tired—no relation to other things. Just happen.

"A long time ago my father brought an espaliered lemon tree all the way from Jamaica," she told him. "It grows in a hot frame and has real lemons. General Jackson loves to suck lemons. They keep you healthy," she said. "It's awful lucky we have them for him, don't you think?"

"Yes, I do indeed," Roan said. "I think that's very lucky."

"My brother Brace," she said, "was a major with Colonel Marron, but he resigned just to be a trooper with Colonel Ashby. That's what we think of Cousin Turner here in the Valley! Will there be a big battle nearby?"

"There'll be a battle, I reckon," he told her solemnly. Not all at once, the way it sounds, but long spells of her talk and Roan answering only when she stopped for him to.

"My sister Thyrza—Brace's wife, that is—hopes her baby is going to be a little boy. I sort of hope it'll be a little girl. Which do you like best? Boys or girls?"

" 'Sugar and spice' "—he bent slightly to her and squeezed her hand—" 'and all things nice.' I reckon I like little girls."

She was silent for a long moment, then her voice was solemn. "I had the right to let my hems out," she said stubbornly. "Black Emmalina is so scared the Yankees'll come, she won't budge from the house, day or night. Can't do anything, unless I tell her what. Brace's wife isn't able to do, until after the baby. Brace isn't here and my father is over with Prince John Magruder. So I have to do. I have to run things." There was quiet pride in it, and a defiant toss of her head. "So if I have the name, I can have the fame, too," she said. "Can't I?" And that wasn't a question, it was pushing her own courage hard from inside, for her voice dropped to softness as she said it. "Besides," she told him, "when my mother died, she told me I'd have to look after my father. That means his house and his people—when he's away too!" She was so near tears that Roan was frightened. Afraid if Molly cried, he'd sit right down on the curb and blubber, too, from a horribly empty sense of the futility of all living. But she didn't cry. She said, "You'll just love General Jackson," and she held up her paper sack of three lemons. "I'll introduce him to you."

There was a crowd in front of Taylor's Hotel and lamplight blazing full, with horse holders steadying the staff mounts on the hitching pole, and suddenly old fat Cap Murt Patton, pushing through with his big red sergeant's chevrons to sleeve and his artillery saber from Mexico banging against his bowed legs. "Roan, I'm pow'ful glad t'see you!"

"Cap Patton, Miss Molly," Roan said. "Cap raised and commanded our comp'ny last year, but he was down Mexico way a war ago with Stonewall—when they were lieutenants and sergeants together. So he got promoted up to headquarters."

"Molly and me, we ole friends, Roan." Cap grinned, and he put a hand on the girl's head. "Lemons," he said. "That's wonderful! He's just come back from suppuh at Doctor Graham's, up the Manse. You go right in, girl. Captain Hotchkiss'll get you to the general." And to the crowd he called hard, "Let the little lady through, y'all y'hear?" Then he grabbed Roan's arm and pulled him back. "All hell's poppin' in the skillet fer breakfast, Roan," he whispered. "Heads'll roll, you mark! Began to happen right after Forney Manigault brought the last batch of newspapers in."

"What?"

"Like-a-this: Gin'ral Jackson pulled his wagons and main body out south with the last of the light, for the benefit of the Yankee scouts to see. To turn 'em fast under cover of darkness and march back again to hit the Yankee off balance and paste him hard, north of town, grace of God and the blessings of the bay'net, like it says in the Bible. But the staff pulled the wrong string. They let his brigades get too far south to come back north again before dawn, and some of the wagons are as far as

Newtown. Eight miles." Cap shook his head. "So we lose the town and the road net."

Roan stared at the old soldier. "You mean we ain't goin' to fight for Winchester, Cap?"

"Lord Harry, Roan!" Cap clutched his arm fiercely. "It ain't Winchester now. It's Richmond—and high, low, jack for the whole cruddy wah!"

"I don't follow that!"

"You ain't paid to. Only himself is paid to. And his own staff got him off balance this time. It'll take a maneuver now to set the Yankees up again. But you'll get yore battle, Roan, when General Jackson's ready foh it! Heah he comes now!"

The provost was clearing the crowd from in front of Taylor's. People were turning away, their lips pursed tight, walking off into the blue darkness, their eyes shadowed in defeat.

Roan never forgot that picture of the man. There General Jackson stood in Taylor's doorway, taller than Roan in his great spurred boots, and the biggest feet you ever saw. Dust brushed clean, but his beard scraggled where he'd tugged an angry hand through it. The visor of his old Institute cap frayed like a cocklebur where his thumb and finger always reached to tug it tight, but never to tug it low enough to cover the flame-blue light of his eyes. Damnedest eyes you ever saw. Like frost-blued fingers poking at you. God in them and the galloping devil. Kindliness and killing. Love and laceration.

He held the paper sack of lemons in one hand and Molly Lentaigne's hand in the other. For a moment, he stood tall and furious as he turned his head back toward the tight, worried faces of his officers behind.

"That," he said, "is the last council of war I will ever hold!" It was soft, but you could hear it all right, for it was like a silken whiplash he cut across their faces. He and Molly came out onto the brick walk.

"But you'll come back to Winchester, general, won't you?"

She looked up at him, clear-eyed, without a vestige of fear in her taut proud little body. His shoulders moved slightly in his own deep tiredness and worry. Then he did a wonderful thing. He smiled and the glory of his great soul was in it. That lumbering, awkward body bent in rough gallantry, and he kissed her hand like a young blade. Roan heard his own knees crack loud as he stood stiff, hand rigid in salute. It's that way with real generals. Just as the true princess felt the rose leaf under a spate of down cushions, a fighting man feels a real general. It's something apart, between man and man, and you can't ever fake it with epaulets and feathers. Tom Jackson was a battle-fighting man!

Going back to the house with Molly, Roan walked stiff against the heavy despair that rode his soul.

"You have a carriage, Molly? Friends south, maybe? Strasburg? Middletown? Nineveh?"

"Oh, yes. Of course. But why?"

"Yore sister's baby," he said quietly.

The little girl stopped. "My father wouldn't like it for us to leave the house and go away. It wouldn't be right, Mr. Catlett."

He held her hand tighter. "You call me Roan," he said. "It's more friendly and we all need comfort tonight. Yore father'd understand, I reckon, with the Yankees coming."

She shook her head. "General Jackson'll come back. I know it, Roan."

"Sure he will. But for now—the baby and all?"

"Well," she said, "I'll ask Thyrza—but she won't leave, I think, unless Brace comes and tells her to. And I won't leave her alone. And what about Mr. Ancrum lying sick? What about Emmalina too scared to move, and old Mordecai too old? Somebody has to watch Doc Tatly close, too, when he's working on a sick horse. He gets talking to them so hard he doesn't watch the bottle."

As they turned into the drive again, there were lights near the house, and horses hoofing the ground. Closer to, one was a milk-white, and Turner Ashby's soft voice challenged them,

"Who is it there?" He hardly came to Roan's shoulder, Turner Ashby, but somehow that didn't matter, for he was a man grown tall in soul. "Catlett," he said, "I've just heard the word we're pulling out south and I've passed it to tell all our boys to rendezvous in Kernstown to screen the infantry withdrawal." Then he saw Molly. He put both gentle hands to her upper arms. "Molly girl," he said soft, "sometimes the Lord God has to have us grow up very fast. Things happen, and He has to make us men and women overnight."

"What is it, Cousin Turner?"

"It's Brace, darling," he said.

"He's hurt? Oh, no!" Her hands went up to the colonel's arms.

"He's—dead, Molly. Killed over Berryville way."

She stood there rigid for a second. You could feel the tightness rack her whole little woman body as she held herself against the horror. Slowly she pressed his hands from her and stood back alone in it. "You haven't—told Thyrza—yet? The way she is?"

"No," Ashby said; "we've just got here."

Her head twisted frantically, looking sharp into the lantern-torn darkness.

"We've taken him inside," Turner Ashby said.

The girl clasped her hands together tightly, twisting them hard against each other. "What shall I do?" she asked him. "What shall I do?"—the soft, frantic age-old wail of woman. No tears yet, only the soul agony to defend the hearthstone. The desperation of all motherhood, seeking within for the courage that is so much deeper than the courage of the firing line—that, in defense of the family, can kill, if need be, so much more ruthlessly than the bayonet. Then, slowly, she turned to Roan. "I can't go away now—even if Thyrza would want to. And she wouldn't."

Turner Ashby took her hand and started for the house, and Forney came out of the darkness. He had Davin's horse saddled for Roan, and his own. He swore in his raw throat and he spat phlegm. "Roan," he said, "we can't leave her here, with the

Yankees comin'. The ole Negra woman's a gibberin' fool and the ole houseman's nigh to ninety and no help at all."

"It's her home," Roan said, "with birth ripenin' in it—and her dead to be buried from it and her father away fightin' with General Magruder. You don't aim to pry a lady away from those lady duties, do you?"

Roan tiptoed in the back to the downstairs bedroom. Davin was sleeping, the heavy breath soughing in his mottled cheeks. Roan took his hand gun and saber and boots, and wrapped them tight in his reeking uniform. He woke Davin up, hand to his forehead to bring him to, easy.

"Davin boy, I'm hidin' yore stuff under the straw in the stable where Jason is. We're pullin' out and Banks' advance guard'll probably be in town tomorrow. You lie doggo and cook a story up how you ain't old enough to jine the army yet, y'hear? You got measles—that'll help prove you ain't grown and keep you from bein' took prisoner. Stay here until we come back."

Davin opened his eyes wide. "We ain't really licked, are we, Roan? God bless, I couldn't stand that!"

Roan closed Davin's door softly and stood for a moment in the hall. From the front of the house he could hear the girl's desperate sobbing, caught inside her with the effort to hold it in control. She was standing at the parlor door, one arm up the side of it, her face pressed tight against the arm. A handkerchief crumpled wet in her other hand. Outside, Roan heard Colonel Ashby's voice calling a soft order; heard horses thrash gravel and trot down the drive, sabers clanking. Roan walked slowly up the long hall. Molly turned at the sound of his footsteps and stared at him in utter desolation. Roan held out his hand for hers, and as she gave it he stooped and kissed her forehead.

Above her on ancient smoky canvas there was a face from long years gone—in Continental regimentals with the pale blue Cincinnati laced in a buttonhole. Beyond her in the parlor there was the same face, dead in youth, with the fierce flame of battle not yet quite shadowed under the calm of death. Trooper Lentaigne, laid decently upon the couch, with his silky blond hair combed and his stiff hands composed upon the hilt of the cavalry saber that lay across him. Between the two, in the anguish of growing up, Molly's tear-stained child's face, with the same delicate pride of nostril and the same full forehead.

"Roan"—she sucked her lip between her teeth and shook her head fiercely—"I am sorry—there was—no supper—for you all," and suddenly she flung herself into his arms. He held her tight against his filthy clothing, giving her what comfort he had to give in her child's need for it. Crying silently inside himself. And against his dirty jacket she whispered, "But I'll take care of Jason, and you tell General Jackson that there'll be more lemons for him when he comes back!" ...

You never see the whole battle from a trooper's saddle. Only that part right around you. All the rest is clouded in rumor, obscured in the fog of war. You never know the plans. Long, long afterward you read what the generals write in books, and some of it becomes clear, but never quite all of it until one day a missing piece turns up when you don't care any more, and the years fall away starkly to your long-dead youth, to cold rain and the white burn of chilblains, to the hard rat gnaw of hunger in your empty belly, to dull hopeless fury in your mind. And you remember, *that's what the newspapers were for.*

Stonewall Jackson's infantry plodded south in silent desolation, with the wagons and what artillery he had, churning the Valley Pike into a thick, cold poultice, knee-deep. Slopping it over onto the bottomless morass of the fields flat beside. White, angry faces, thin-lipped and bitter in the eyes. Newtown to Strasburg to Woodstock, and Jackson himself as far as Rude's Hill. Slow, slogging, hungry miles with odds of eight to one—some will put it ten to one—at their backs. Retreating. Giving ground. Their own Valley land, where their hopes lived and their dead lay buried in the old churchyards.

Rumor lashed the army of the Valley for ten febrile days like a gaunt old harridan with a bitter tongue. Johnston east, across the Blue Ridge, was falling back too—to the Rapidan River. The Rapidan, hell! Johnston's headed way back toward the Virginia Central Rail Road line. The Pamunkey River line. The gates to Richmond. Against McClellan's quarter million new army thrusting out of Washington, the Southern armies were rolling up like a tattered tent cloth. The jig's up and the fiddler's goin' home ....

The Yankees were in Winchester for a while, feeling south after Jackson. Feeling easy, for they knew he was done. *Piquet* brawling only. Tantalizing. Dusting up Ashby's scouting cavalry. Then the brawling fell off to nothing and the Yankees pulled back into Winchester. Soon the most of them began to move out east to Castleman's Ferry across the Shenandoah, heading for Snicker's Gap through the Blue Ridge Mountains to pour more pressure on Johnston. Why? *Why,* if McClellan's quarter million is over there pushing Johnston already? Ask Stonewall Jackson—but ask him fast, for that night he turned his columns. And now it's gospel that he suspected all along that McClellan wasn't there—a word here, an item there, something somewhere else in those newspapers he pored over every night—and troops leaving Winchester for the east proves it! So turn right about, for Jackson starts before dawn always—unless he starts in the middle of the night. Force the infantry march back north to Winchester—forty-three miles in two days, with having to pull each foot free from twelve inches of glutinous sucking, spring-flood Virginia, each step north. Stonewall Jackson for the Valley, with a battle comin' up!

Kernstown, friend? Got licked sure 'nuff. But to no frazzle, sir—*not* to no frazzle.

Turner Ashby hit the Yankee rearguard *piquets* on their east flank a mile south of Winchester, out of Kernstown, like a roaring Valley storm lashing down the Massanuttons. Hit 'em with two hundred and eighty hell-for-tarnation cavalrymen and three little horse guns to develop the battle for General Jackson.

General Jackson moved the infantry off the Pike west to fight the main action, maneuvering across Middle Road toward the Opequon and the Cedar Creek Turnpike, grace of God and the blessings of the bay'net.

One time, Turner Ashby and his cavalrymen cut their way plumb into the streets of Winchester on the blade. Right straight into the yard of the Lentaigne house, and there was Davin Ancrum bustin' out of the barn with that great golden horse to bridle, yellin', "Git off m'hoss, Roan! This yere's yourn!" draggin' at Roan's near leg to pull him down.

Young Molly shouted from the veranda, "It's Brace's horse, Roan! Her name's Lady!" And then softly to Roan alone as he pulled up under the veranda rail: "She's got Timoleon's blood in her too"—and again: "Jason couldn't get well. Doc Tatly knew, the second day. So I did it, Roan, with Brace's gun. In the ear, Roan. Close. I kissed him for you first. He never knew." Then very softly, "I thought you'd like for me to do it. Not doc." And in the yard, reaching for his stirrup, "It was a boy, Roan—Thyrza's baby. He's Brace Lentaigne now," and, as Roan kneed fast away, "You'll come—back—Roan—someday, please?"

Then Ashby rallied his raid and they cut out of Winchester again, closing in on Jackson's right to press the main fight two miles south of town. Up near Pritchard's Hill they were at it with the bay'net, some of the Virginia companies worn thin enough to spit the survivors on one ramrod, but they fought it out cold to sundown, and withdrew in decent order from the field. And that was the Kernstown fight.

So long, long afterward it's all written down in the books the generals write—how McClellan wasn't east of the Blue Ridge at all, but gone by water to attack Richmond up the Peninsula. And the books say that when Lincoln received the report of Kernstown, he stopped the tail end of the movement at once, for fear of a counterthrust on Washington, so that on the eve of

McClellan's advance up the Peninsula to Richmond, he found himself suddenly deprived of the whole 1st Army Corps.

So the fight wasn't Kernstown at all. Eighty dead men up there in the Shenandoah Valley lost their lives to save Richmond. And that's a bargain.

But not yet, you're not old. Not yet. There is Stonewall still in the living flesh that night, with the sadness of another battle fought on Sunday riding his godly soul. Standing roadside, his long coat loose-draped from his hunched shoulders, his great fingers twined behind his back, nursing the hand hit at Manassas, staring into the glow of the spitting log fire, as the returns of battle are brought to him.

"I think I may say that I am satisfied, sir," he said, and after another moment, he rubbed his hands briskly and walked slowly off into the darkness.

Still later, with Lady standing to hand for the brush and a sackful of oats, the things that Molly had said came alive to Roan again and echoed down from the stars. As if she were right there beside him saying them now: "I kissed him for you first. He never knew. I thought you'd like for me to do it. Not doc."

Davin, wrapped tight against the chill, looked across at Forney and reached a hand for a drag at Forney's pipe. Forney grinned. "Wonder what the Yankee newspapers'll say tomorrow?"

"Never mind that," Davin said. "I got to get the straight of something else. I ain't sayin' anything about the little girl. She nursed me fine. But what happened to the young lady that met us at the stable door? Sick as I was, I could see she was powerful pretty—and awful worth knowin' fer her presence and manners—and not bein' afraid."

Roan looked across at him. "You ain't goin' to see that young lady again," he said, "for four more years. Because it's goin' to take her that long to get to be sixteen. And you ain't goin' to see her then, Mistuh Ancrum, because I aim to call on her m'self, and take her hoss back. Does that answer yore question, sir?"

Roan Catlett rode Lady for the rest of the war. You cannot speak of a mare like Lady for, like a fine woman, she was what she was only to Roan. The Short Mountain Cavalry Company kept its identity as long as Turner Ashby lived, but with the attrition of campaign it gradually disintegrated and its members were absorbed in other units. Forney Manigault and Davin Ancrum were Roan's men throughout, and where he went they went too. And they went the route.

From the doubtful victory of Kernstown, Jackson withdrew deep into the Valley, drawing Banks after him as water seeks its level, rather than inspiring Banks with a retreating target for hot pursuit. Banks was a politician primarily and a general only through opportunity. He fought his battles on letter paper to his superiors in Washington, filling them full of campaign pledges which he seldom attempted to carry out. Jackson fought his in advance, in the lone and secret recesses of his professional mind.

By the end of April, Strasburg, Winchester, Front Royal, New Market, and Harrisonburg were choked with Union Troops, The lower Valley was solid with Banks' Army—twenty thousand men, with Blenker, Geary, and Abercrombie near enough to the railroad to reinforce him by steam car, with sixteen thousand more. Across the Shenandoah Mountains to the west, was Frémont's Union Army with the mission of making junction with Banks through the passes— about nine thousand more men. Eighty miles to the east, across the Blue Ridge Mountains, McDowell at Fredericksburg had thirty-three thousand Federal troops opposing Anderson's twelve thousand Confederates for the northern drive on Richmond while McClellan lay to the southeast of the Confederate capital with one hundred and ten thousand men, against Joe Johnston's fifty thousand.

Simplify it: one hundred and forty-three thousand Union troops directly threatened Richmond, with sixty-two thousand Confederates to defend on April 30th, 1862.

In the Valley, Jackson, with a total available force of seventeen thousand, was faced with a junction of two Union armies totalling forty-five thousand, all told. If he left the Valley, it was lost to the Confederacy and if he did not time his leaving right, McDowell might cut him off with thirty-three thousand more before he could reach Richmond.

It has been the lot of most American soldiers in modern times to fight winning wars. Victory, or the instinctive knowledge of victory to come, is an incentive that transcends fear and dysentery, jungle heat and bitter cold, hunger, wounds, and the raw, gaunt lot of the individual soldier. He goes on in vision of the bright end to his going.

Few armies have been magnificent in defeat. Washington's tattered rabble crossing Jersey. The British regulars whipped from Mons to the Marne. The young men of Korea.

And Jackson's men of April '62.

It is a gauge of Jackson that he never made a plan without first basing it on the best possible knowledge he could obtain of the enemy situation. Throughout history, it is a recurring phenomenon that even the greatest generals have had the unfortunate habit of mind of entertaining firm convictions of what the enemy would do and thereafter accepting all indications that proved them right, rejecting all that proved them wrong. Napoleon was guilty twice, of record. Once at Moscow. Once at Waterloo. In our time such cumulative mistakes were made twice. Once at Pearl Harbor. Once at Bastogne.

But Jackson was a superb-G-2. He knew Banks' character and he knew that Banks' immediate striking force of twenty thousand men was twenty miles north of Staunton—six march hours by the roads of that day. If Banks joined Frémont, the jig was up. The junction was imminent.

If there is any cardinal rule of tactics, which one doubts—it being an involved and almost an exact science—it is to strike before forces are joined full, or once joined, to divide them by maneuver and defeat them in detail. Piecemeal.

Jackson chose not to await the junction. He saw his opportunity and took it in one of the boldest, most carefully-thought-out moves in military history. But to make it dead certain, he put the fatal quietus on Banks first. He pulled the wool over the joker's eyes in as magnificent a maneuver as the realm of counter-intelligence records. He cost Banks six hours' march time by bluffing deuces against Banks' three of a kind and Banks believed him.

So did Jackson's soldiers, and the heart went out of some of them. It went out of Roan Catlett and a little bit of Roan died within him. For there is no such thing as a brave man or a steadfast man. Some are more continuously brave and steadfast than others, but with most men these qualities fluctuate within the confines of their basic characters. Character itself is a template within which there are certain general things a man will or will not do—within which there are certain prices he will not pay, or accept.

Courage in war attains to certain levels within each individual. He will, as a general rule, move forward with his unit when the order comes. Not to, is to invoke drastic and public penalty. He will, when forced to act alone and without witnesses, tend to doubt the incumbent necessity for full-out effort, and consider his own hide as of primary importance. Again, there is a certain madness right around the corner of every combat soldier's mind. He lives in personal filth and privation. He has, if he is lucky in mind, drawn the curtain close behind him so that he no longer hears the throaty whisper of his girl or sees the lights of home at dusk. He has had to close himself to the past in order to free his present of ghosts that might betray his necessity for alertness. But a curtain is also drawn ahead of him. Just beyond the immediate. For he has no future. He lives with death; therefore he is free to court her. And sometimes madness takes his mind, the Death Wish flames full and he trades

the last vestige of sanity for the primeval killing, the hate of instinctive aeons—and his Ultimate Discharge.

If this were not so, there would be no difference between the
worth of decorations. It is significant that the citations for the
highest are beyond the comprehension of most combat veterans.
It is more significant that they are given posthumously, more often
than not.

Somewhere between these levels, Roan fluctuated, when
Jackson left the Valley.

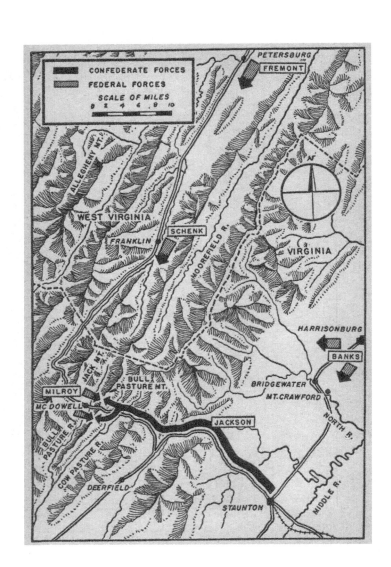

HOW STONEWALL
CAME BACK

IT WAS TOWARD the last of that second April that Roan Catlett began to ride in the shadow of black doubt. The bright Manassas fight of the summer before had tarnished dull under the slow months of falling back to the Rappahannock. In the Shenandoah Valley, Jackson, heavily outnumbered, played fox most of the time, but all the time he'd given ground. From the Potomac patrols, he'd been pushed south to Winchester, only to give up Winchester and pull farther south. With only Ashby's scattered cavalry actions pressuring back on the Northern pursuit and the eternal sharp picket brawls, to give the feeling of any fight left in it at all. Once there had been that brilliant countermarch back to Winchester, for the Kernstown Fight. Forty-three muddy miles of marching back—for a three-hour slug fight and out south once more, proud, but licked again!

The sawdust runs out of a man and he becomes old inside, with an old man's senile fears close to his heart and an old man's tears drenching his soul. Inside, where he lived, Roan was licked. It hung on him night and morning and wouldn't lift, whatever. Too close to his personal honor to say the word, but too insistent now, to give it the lie.

That last morning in April when General Turner Ashby sabered the Union cavalry back into their own camps at Harrisonburg, it came plain to Roan. There ain't no use. You could always drive them in, in small actions, but still they came acoming. From Harrisonburg north, the Valley was choked thick with Yankees. Solid blocked to the Potomac. Across the Shenandoah Mountains due west, there was Frémont's brand-new Western Army, rumored to come down through Buffalo Gap and take Staunton. Behind Roan's back, across the Blue Ridge Mountains east, there were thirty-three thousand Federals pressing Fredericksburg, to close the northern door on McClellan's siege of Richmond—and if that ain't all four sides but a footpath, what is?

Ashby brought his troopers out of the woods after re-forming them and led them back down the Cross Keys Road toward Port Republic. They said Turner Ashby'd gone a little mad a year ago when they killed his brother. Said when Dick Ashby's body was lowered into the grave up at Romney that Turner had snapped his brother's saber across his knee and thrown both pieces in on the casket. Said the two broken pieces striking hollow wood was worse than any curse he might have called. Strange man. Small and dark almost to a Spanish cast. Praying man. Gentle in his words and clean in talk and thought. A man'd do well not to have Ashby's hand against him.

Warm rain soaked them, running down inside, washing the body filth into their steaming boots. Roan felt it good. Miserable—but perversely good—a part of the whole damned business under the mists that hid the great hulking mountains like veils across the faces of mourning women.

If they killed my brother Buford, I'd never let up on 'em. But I saved Bufe from it for a couple of years till he gets eighteen— and it ain't goin' to last that long. Bufe don't die trailside with the outer air blood-bubblin' through a hole in his chest, pressuring his lungs to slow strangulation. No, sir; he stays at V.M.I. down in Lexington where a drill gun in hand'll give him the feel and a uniform to his back'll lend the cockiness. When pa wrote he'd tried to leave school and enlist, I wrote it strong to Bufe, like deserting his corps. Job was plain. Study and work it out for two more years. No, sir, Bufe, a man don't run away from the job in hand. He works it out to the finish, before he takes on the next.

Roan skinned his lips back off his teeth in violent mental satisfaction. Bufe was his—out of all the family. Bufe was his own, in some strange way it can happen. There had always been thoughts and laughter between them without words. A piece of the cosmos, divided equally. Each knowing the inner man of the other since the very beginning, when Bufe, toddling on fat uncertain legs, walked from his mother and put his chubby hand in Roan's four-year-old one. "Let go m'brother! I do his fightin' for him, 'till he grows!"

Morning of May first it was still raining. Not in drops you could see, but in heavy drenching sheets that brushed your face like gossamer wash on God's clothesline. The threadbare head of General Jackson's column came up the Elk Run Valley out of that rain, six thousand all told, but sullen inside from retreating. Men slogging mud to the knees in places, guns bogging down to trunnions, until they were dug free. Horses' legs plastered with the drying mud on their backs corded thick like scabs over saber cuts. But the column didn't cross the Shenandoah into Port Republic town. It turned east on the Brown's Gap Road, heading for the Blue Ridge Mountains.

You couldn't believe that, when you first saw it from Ashby's bivouac. Must be one regiment turning off to secure that side of the crossing, while the rest went on into town. Only it wasn't. Regiment after regiment made the same turn east and the column didn't stop for even a breath. Mechum's Station lay that way— on the Virginia Central Rail Road—with Richmond south and east by steam car. And all the Valley left behind. Harrisonburg, Staunton, Lexington—for the Yankees to pour into if Jackson left. And Jackson was leaving.

You could see the infantry sucking the greasy mud, feel the misty mountains pawing at your shoulders, but you couldn't hear above the snarling river water, whiteroaring, so that you had to shout, "What's that?"

"The Valley jig is up! Jackson's pulling out for the last stand around Richmond. March direction don't lie. He's headin' for the rail road and it's high-low-jack and the game!"

A few minutes later Turner Ashby was crouching roadside with his map on his knee, his milk-white horse beside him, laced thick with the mud. General Ashby hated to have his horse streaked, but there wasn't time. There never was time any more. He had his orders.

He passed them. "The main screen will be maintained on Harrisonburg," he said softly, "to cover the rear of General Jackson's withdrawal. Two troops will work well over west, and north of Staunton to fend around Buffalo Gap, Lebanon Springs, McDowell and the Bull Pasture River, to feel out the advance elements of General Frémont's Shenandoah Mountain Army." Ashby looked up at the handful of his officers and non-coms. There was mud in his black mustache, twisted into it like pomade, but his dark eyes were as calm as if he were planning to plow his north forty, up at Rose Hill. "Those two troops will be between two Federal armies," he said, "so don't go to shooting up each other through jumpiness. The orders are to fend and scout"—Turner Ashby folded his map and stood up—"and delay fighting where you can without being sucked in and taken. Questions?"

There it was, plain. The last muddy ditch! Throw the cavalry back against them once again to hide the fact of withdrawal as long as possible. Nine hundred of Ashby's troopers against two Federal armies. Feel 'em, fool 'em. fuddle 'em, as long as could be to let Jackson get to Richmond. Stonewall's heart must be broken inside him at the orders calling him down there—and every other Valley heart with it.

Roan's troop rode west for two days. Back toward Cross Keys and down to Bridgewater. Mount Crawford and on to Stabling's Spring. He didn't want to get out of this dreadful break-up alive somehow, and yet he didn't want to die. He'd built up too much credit on the living side. Other men right and left had been killed riding with him and he had lived. To die now was like throwing in a good hand at cards. But there wouldn't be anything to live for afterwards, if you played 'em. The money wouldn't buy. You couldn't even get the last year out of mind, and with the war lost, you couldn't tolerate the awful memory. It would be like the cancerous lumps that grow inside of old folks. Can't cut them out, so they snarl their growing into vitals until the only way left is death. Death becomes academic and the values of life cease to be.

The third day, when they had a sharp skirmish along Mossy Creek with a Harrisonburg vedette, Roan fought with his whole mind and body waiting for a bullet. Hell, it couldn't be long now. There wa'n't nothing left but for it to hit him. He began to quiver in his flesh for it, like a horse twitching flies, and when the fight was done, he had a bad five or ten minutes when he thought he was going to cry—go all to pieces and whimper in his soul. He clawed his sweating face with his dirty fingers. Twisted his hands into it for control. His breath caught in silent sobs and he had no God in that moment to lean upon, because he felt unworthy to call upon Him. It was like he had really died a little bit and was halfway across. Too far to pull clear back and not far enough to go on. Awful.

The troop moved on up into North River Gap in the Shenandoahs, and Roan rode with it like a man in sick stupor. There were almost four troops in the mountains by May sixth, under Ashby's Captain Sheetz. Operating by squads and half troops, feeling out the road to Franklin for General Frémont's advance guard—fending as far north as Brock's Gap Settlement to make sure Frémont wouldn't try to come through the mountains up there to join his army with Banks' at Harrisonburg, instead of south to take undefended Staunton. Roan didn't care what happened. His heart was gone out of it.

He knew he was going home a couple of days before he went. Not deserting, for there was nothing left to desert from—just going home, like a man has to when his work's finished, win or lose. Plugging these mountains, just waiting for it, hopelessly, was fool's business now, with Jackson gone. Sure you could spot 'em first and sting 'em like always, but four troops couldn't stop Frémont. Frémont's army would pour through four troops like spring wash down the creeks and there'd be nothing left but lost hope. But today, tomorrow, there was still time and everything'd be the same at home as before—except in his mind. At least he'd have that sameness to breathe in for a spell, before it happened.

The Catlett place was about six miles from Deerfield in the Short Mountain country. Log cabin it was in Indian times long before. Then built onto as they cleared the land in his great-grandfather's time and more still in his grandfather's. When the Tidewater branch of Catletts died out, the old English furniture and the silver came over the mountains by oxcart, and some of the Catlett pictures came with it. That was when they built the brick part of the house. Funny hodgepodge of a place really, because the Catletts never tore any of the old parts down. They just built on solidly as they lived solidly. Kept what they had and added to. The women they married did that for them—kept the blood and kept the progression.

It wasn't that Roan really wanted to go home, because he really didn't. There just wasn't anything left for him to do. It was going to hurt bad to go, because he'd have to tell his father all of it and he hated to do that. How they'd whipped the Yankees man for man and troop for troop, every time the fight was joined—and yet lost it all somehow day by day, week by week, until nothing was left now but a handful of tired and ragged cavalrymen in the mountains, between two whole Yankee armies—with Richmond ringed about and the Valley wide open. *Thy will be done—but dear God in heaven, I wish I was a little boy again with my father big to help me.*

Roan hadn't ever wanted to go home since he'd started out for Harper's Ferry last year. He seemed to have a soldier's instinct about that from the start. Turn your back on all that was before and don't come back until the fight's over or it'll weaken you somehow in your mind. It'll soften your bowels against going back to fear and sweat and killing.

He walked slowly down the Green Valley Pike, leading his tired mare, Lady, and breathing the evening air deep for the first smell of his own chimney smoke. Lady touched her velvet lips to his crusted shoulder, slobbered his upper arm and breathed down her nose in soft whispers to him. Frémont's men'd burn the houses and loot off the stuff to send north. A trooper of Ashby's they'd collar like a hoss thief, like as not hang him where they took him. But not Roan. That's what a man's last gunload is for, to shoot it out cold to them for his own kill, standing. He ground his teeth in tired and impotent rage, for all the dead men he'd buried and all the hope that had died with them, for his youth that was gone and his old age that would never sit upon him more heavily than it did this night.

Then roadside, half a dozen yards ahead to the right, a gun-lock snicked open sharp. "Stand and stipulate!" Roan stopped in his tracks. It was an old man's voice, cracked slightly in the words, but not with fear—and the sound of it echoed vaguely from the past.

"Friend," Roan said, puzzling the voice.

"Friend to who?"

Roan laughed then. "Friend to Judge Manigault," he said, "and to Gin'ral Turner Ashby and Stonewall Jackson! That enough, sir? I'm Roan Catlett, judge."

"God bless m'soul, Roan"—the judge stepped out of the rhododendron. "H'are you, boy?" and with his old Lefevre rifle in his left hand, he held out his right to Roan. "Yore pappy'll shore be glad t'see you!"

"Yes, sir," Roan said. "Yore boy Forney's all right, last I saw. He's up around Harrisonburg, with Ashby himself."

"Oh, Forney'll get along," the judge snorted. "The Slow Devil's in him and the Devil always looks after his own." He swept an arm back toward the roadside and two more armed figures crawled out of the bushes. One was Tom Ruffin, the hunchback saddle maker from Deerfield, and the other was Davin Ancrum's eleven-year-old brother, Custis. They had rifles, and white kerchiefs were tied to their upper left arms.

"What is it?" Roan asked.

"Law of levée, suh," Judge Manigault said. "Legal as taxes. We heard things weren't turnin' off good just right now and that this yere fellow Frémont was on his way down yere from Franklin with a brand-new Yankee Army to join Banks. Folks don't take kindly to John C. Frémont heahabouts, even though his wife is Senator Tom Benton's daughter, Jessie—grand-niece to Governor McDowell, of Cherry Grove, just south a piece. Bad blood, suh! His mother was Miz' Anne Whiting Pryor, who left her husband in Richmond and ran off to Savannah with a schoolteacher named Frémont, his father. Major Pryor should've shot the seducer dead, you ask me, but the major was an old man with a shaky hand. So we aim to shoot the son, he sets foot in our country!"

"You can't," Roan said; "a citizen fires a shot at a blue-coat, they'll execute him out of hand."

"No, suh." Judge Manigault drew himself up. "Law of *levée en masse*, suh. All the old men left—all the boys too young to go. They ain't firin' any lone, personal shots at Frémont. That's *franc-tireurin'*—not legal. But *levée en masse* is legal as militia. These yere handkerchiefs on our arms and the feathers in our caps is uniform. Every man jack of the Short Mountain Defense Comp'ny has stood up and sworn to obey me—a regularly sittin' magistrate of the Commonwealth of Virginia, suh. That's command. Uniform and command make us an armed force under the law of *levée en masse*, same as the army, suh—and as we stand—not a one of Frémont's men's goin' to come into our mountain or our valley and live to talk about it!"

"You tell Davin you saw me, Roan," young Custis Ancrum said. "You tell him pappy and me ain't goin' to let 'em burn our house and barns!"

The tears were so thick in Roan's throat that he choked. "Well——" he said. "Well, I reckon——"

"Git along, boy," Judge Manigault told him. "You'll be late t'yore suppah."

A mile farther down, Roan turned in the drive and led Lady straight to the barn.

There was lantern light up there and after a moment it raised high. "Who is it?"

Roan stopped and swallowed hard, "Roan, sir," and the two men stood there, twenty yards apart across the darkness, unable to move for a minute or to say more. What can be said, ever, between a grown man and his father? That they both lived once, drawn close in child love and love of child, and that the years have broken the protecting circle so that no longer can arms fend danger or a son in manhood seek them? Of the hour before the attack, when the need for older words and thought becomes so vital, that it is a pain inside like unto nausea? Or of the older man, roaming the cold house with the haunt upon him, when the rain beats with the high wind off Short Mountain? *Take care of yourself, Roan*—like a hoarse, demanding prayer.

Their hands came together, more to keep each from embracing the other than for any other reason, and Thomas Catlett said, "You've thickened through, Roan," and Roan said, "Reckon so," and that was awful, for there was so much more they couldn't say. "Go to your mother, boy. I'll do for the hoss," and Roan said, "Yes, sir"; then he was running blind toward the house, his boots and spurs thundering across the summer-kitchen breezeway and up the steps in back. "Mom!"

He scrubbed himself clean in the great wooden tub in the kitchen and got into clean clothing and it felt wrong on him somehow, like a popinjay strutting uniform in the Richmond Home Guard. It took him back to times before—and there never could be times before—ever again. His campaign smell was gone to his own nostrils and his honor somehow gone with it.

"What's it like, Roan? Do they give you warm food? Do you have chapel service?" The searching, homely questions of mothers, against the things they cannot know.

"Not like yore cooking, mom"—he tried to smile, but the effort twisted his mouth hard—"and not like the Revrund Kinsolving's brimstone preaching."

"What's it like, Roan?"—his sister, Emily, turned fifteen, intense and slendering tall, with burgeoning womanhood. "What's it like, Roan!"—breathless with it almost, as she held his boots, new dubbined by her own hand in fierce love for her older brother. *Tell me of the gallantry and the glory and of some young Lochinvar I cannot yet know, but who rides for me as surely as my heart beats for the sound of hoofs that will someday come. What's it like, Roan?* Her eyes were bright upon him with her delicate nostrils flared to her indrawn breath.

"Boredom mostly, Em. Hurry up—and wait. And measles." He laughed to stem the tears within, for the knowledge was full upon him that his own people were utter strangers to him this night. That what had been so close a part of him was no longer there for him to touch. The year between was like a wall between. The voices he knew so well could not probe his thinking any more. Like a man in a dream he was, who walks eternally through a blank-faced crowd, trying to ask for that which he must seek, with his voice soundless, and deaf ears turned against him.

"What's it like, Roan?" Charlie looked up at him with his chubby boy's face turning man subtly with his tenth year, his eyes wide and his jaw pushed out hard. "You kill a lot of Yankees, Roan? Tell us how!"

Edward half drew his saber and touched a thumb to the cutting edge. "Ask pop, Roan; if I can join the levée. Custis Ancrum's only seven months older than me. Ask him!" ...

"What's it like, Roan?" That was his father, much later, when Sarah Catlett left them together with a woman's instinct for a man and his first son. It had a different sound from all the others, as if somehow Thomas Catlett knew what it was like full well, but didn't dare to do any more about it than ask. Roan stood up and walked across behind the table, wondering how to tell it; knowing he had to, but wondering how. Then he knew how the only way must be.

"I don't know about Richmond, sir, but we've lost the Valley cold. Gin'ral Jackson's had to pull out at last. Left only Ashby."

"Yes"—his father frowned slightly—"I was afraid so, from what we heard." He nodded once or twice, like a man who finally gets his thinking straight.

"They've sent us over here," Roan said, "four thin troops, to do what we can to harass Frémont joining Banks. That's the story plain"—he shook his head fiercely—"and it's no use!"

"What then, Roan?" his father asked softly.

There it was as Roan had dreaded it. He was the man bringing the news—the man with the immediate experience. He posed the problem. His, then, to make the decision, for it is too late ever to be a little boy again, once the years have passed.

"I don't know, sir," he said helplessly. "What do you think?"

"I don't know," Thomas Catlett said. "You've got older than me, somehow, Roan, since you went off with the army. You know things I don't know. Think things, I reckon, that have never been in my mind. I have never been a soldier, Roan. It is as if I were suspended somehow between Grandfather Catlett and you. Somewhere between Cowpens and Yorktown in that old war and General Jackson in this one. Looking in through a window. Not a part of it." Thomas Catlett smiled wistfully. "It is as if you were my father, in a way; not I yours."

Roan drew in a deep breath. "I'll tell you then, sir"—and the shame was full upon him, but he beat it back with the heavy hand of youth. "We must load the wagons with all we want to save, and take the family out south. Mother and Emily and the two boys."

The words were there between them, and there was no calling them back. Their echo lay in shattered pieces, jagged and ugly with destruction, and the silence that followed after was the silence of things dead.

"Out south—to where, Roan?"

"I don't know," Roan said. "All I know is that the Valley jig is up and I had to come and tell you."

The silence fell again, and it was a dreadful-sounding nothingness that hung in the old room and probed the farthest reaches of its shadows. From the walls, it came back upon them again like tide returning up the beach and held them in its cold import of finality.

"What about Buford, down at Lexington?" His father's voice was steady.

Then it was as if Roan had known all along that his father would ask that question next. As if he had been standing, braced, to meet it, but when it came he had no answer.

"How is Bufe?" he asked quickly. "Have you heard? Tell me!" Too quickly, to buy him time.

Thomas Catlett moved his eyes to look at his oldest son without moving his head. "Last week," he said, "Buford wrote you had written him about not leaving school"—and that was all Thomas Catlett said. For just a second or two his tongue sucked his lips as if he would say more, but he closed his mouth on the impulse and clasped his hands on the table edge. The words he might have said were in Roan's mind, plainer than if he had said them: *Like deserting your corps, Bufe—a man don't run away from the job in hand. He works it out to the finish before he takes on the next.* Deep anger lashed at Roan's vitals, caught as he was between necessity and the shame of meeting it. He was like a man tied up and struck, then, across the face. You couldn't tell this to Buford, for Buford couldn't know it yet for what it really was. He was like Roan had been last year—fresh in his heart for it, eager with the dreams of childhood, but with manhood bursting within him now to make those dreams come true. The trap of glory. The bone-strewn short cut that eternally weaves its bloody snare for youth.

"You know that boy better than I do, Roan," his father said. "His heart is one with your heart. Where you are is where his mind lives. What you do is what he will always try to follow. You might be twins—close in mind as some twins are. But with more than that in it, because you are older. Older enough so that all of Buford's life you will be to him what a father is for the first few years of a boy's life. His god, Roan."

Then the guilt came full upon Roan and hung in his nostrils like the stench of flesh rot. Not his own guilt alone but the guilt of despair that creeps into the souls of men as sickness will take their bodies when plague stalks the land. Rotting their minds with the mass fear that comes of doubt and question. Shriveling their hearts until they are like sheep for the driving, denying them the right to walk in forthright pride as men, destroying the heritage of God's image.

Thomas Catlett reached a steady hand and raised his brandy to his lips. He watched his son's eyes over the rim of the glass as he drank. "What were you planning—to drop by Lexington on the way? To tell Buford and take him along—on south?"

Roan stared at the older man. "I—a——"

Just then the dogs began to give voice down in the runs. Old Bess first, with her heavy bell ringing full to the night. Then the others waking and coming in on the chorus because it was Old Bess and they didn't dare not take her word for whatever stalked the darkness. Close in to the house Splinter woke and growled in his whitening muzzle, like an old man cursing for the sleep he was going to lose now. Roan stepped quickly for his hand gun, pulled it out of holster.

His father watched him for a moment, then he crossed to the door, opened it and stepped outside. Splinter was growling down by the pike now, thrashing angrily around through the brush, circling for what scent there would be to satisfy his sleepwalking. Outside with his father, the darkness seemed to bring the whole place in close on Roan. To ring him about tightly so that he couldn't move his arms. There was too much of it suddenly for one man to live in all alone. Too many old people crowding close for a moment, whispering from other years long gone. Buckskin people with long rifles to hand who had known Captain Washington long before General Braddock got to know him—or My Lord Cornwallis. Steady people, forthright to God and stouthearted to living with the fundamentals deep grained in their souls. It was like they had all slowly drifted down from the burial place to stand by this night and watch the Catletts close—with the right the Catletts have to watch their own. Babies born in the old house, who had grown up to those mountains, to call the land theirs in their time—in sweat and worry and heartbreak. In joy and loving and living. The gun hung heavy in Roan's hand, like someone pulling on his arm, and in that moment he knew his shame full.

"There is someone on the pike," his father said quietly. They could see old Splinter against the night sky. He had straightened out his circling and was standing braced with his ancient nose up to what wind there was. Then Old Bess in the runs must have told him, for she tore it out of her throat suddenly to shout the others down in a panic of unholy joy and Splinter took off up the road fit to tear his rheumatism out by the roots.

"Lord a'mighty!" Buford said. "Ain't it enough I got to walk all night but Judge Manigault like to shot me down the road, Splinter like to eat me up and m'own brother Roan meets me gun in hand!... H'are you, dad?... Damn, man, I'm glad t'see you, Roan! What time is it?" And again there the three of them were as Roan and his father had been earlier, with so much to say and no words to say it with. No power to get it out of their inner thinking.

"Past eleven, Buford," Thomas Catlett said.

"Just made it," Buford snorted in disgust, "in time to turn around and mosey straight back!"

"Made it from where, Bufe?" Roan's voice was sharp.

"Staunton, Roan. Where else?"

"What the hell for Staunton!"

"Well——" Buford grinned. "The army must of done something wrong, for they sent word for the Cadet Corps to come on up from the Institute to help. We left Lexington the first of May to march up. General Smith marched us—they say to General Jackson's order. That's all I know."

"That can't be!" Roan said helplessly. "They wouldn't do that—put boys in to hold Staunton!"

"Not so much of the boy talk, Roan," Buford grinned. "They gave us men's shoes and socks down at the Deaf and Dumb Asylum where we're camped, and we're going to get real rifles to replace our smooth bores when we take off west to fight Frémont." He stood on one foot and held up the other to show the issue shoes. His cadet trousers were stuffed in mud-crusted laced leggings and his short jacket was strapped at the waist with the Institute belt—buckle turned to the rear. "Too bright for a target," he said. "Orders are to wear it in back, but polish it bright, don't fear!" and he pulled the Institute *képi* down to his eyes so's just not to hide them, in the selfsame way General Jackson had of doing, and Roan knew suddenly that every man jack of the corps was doing just that to his *képi* forty times a day, because Jackson had that habit, hoping to burr the visor with thumb and finger just as Jackson's was burred. Of such things are schoolboys made forever—and were it not so, there would be no men in the world.

"What you doin' here, Roan? They told us Ashby was screening way up in the mountains. Towards Franklin."

"That's right," Roan growled. "I—just—dropped by. Close enough to."

"Me, too," Buford said. "Got a pass 'til reveille. Reckon I should see ma? Or would it upset her—me havin' to go right back without even time for a snack?"

"Reckon you should," his father said. He stood for a moment looking full at his oldest son in what light there was, and a strange thing came to pass. Just as Thomas had felt for a brief moment that Roan was older in his mind than he was in his for this night, so now Buford, as he stood there slightly puzzled, looking from one to the other, was older than either of them, for manhood isn't years, it is heart, and if the heart be strong in youthful dreams, who shall deny that it still is heart?

"I'll go saddle Lady," Roan growled. He walked across the paddock, icy cold in his whole inner body. How could they do it? How could they order those boys up from Lexington to try to hold Staunton, when Jackson's whole army had pulled out? His fury snarled in his mind like a treed hill cat—the numb fury a soldier lives in half his time. He cursed General Jackson with his lips drawn thin against his teeth. *They cannot have Buford. I'll go back, but they cannot have Buford.* But he knew now he was only whistling in the dark. Had been, about Bufe, from the first.

When he led Lady up to the house, his mother stood there with a handkerchief crushed tightly in her hand, but no tears. "It seems a shame," she said, "to walk so far to have to start right back! I'll give you some ham and biscuits to take. I——"

"It's only fifteen miles up and fifteen back," Buford said, "by road. Shorter the way I cut across. It's nothing—as long as I saw you for a minute. And none of you are to worry," he said solemnly, "because Frémont ain't goin' to get to pass through those mountains! Take my word for it. *Virginiae Fidem Praesto!*"

Thomas Catlett took down his squirrel rifle. "I'll walk a piece back with you both."

Then they were on the road again north. Three shadowy figures with Lady behind, following Roan close for comfort. The night damp was down full and there was still no talk in it, for there couldn't be. The thinking ran too deep for talk. Old thinking. That these three men were not themselves alone, but only a part of a long dead march behind them to bring them where they were tonight. And that ahead in the shadows of tomorrow lay the further march of their own sons. Caught between, the present tenants of the name, with the power in their hearts to add to it, but no right whatsoever to detract.

After a while Thomas Catlett stopped and pulled a white kerchief from his pocket, circling his upper left arm with it and knotting it with his teeth.

"Judge Manigault's road block is just beyond," he said. "I've got the twelve-to-daylight watch with Doctor Crosset and Senator Ancrum. Good night, boys." He held out his hand to Roan.

Roan stared at his father. "You just let me talk! You weren't goin', whatever!"

"I reckon not," his father smiled. "This Valley is mine—from way back. I wouldn't—have any other place to go." Roan took his father's hand and then he whipped off his hat and leaned and kissed his father's cheek. Bufe took off his hat. Thomas took off his hat. "Take care of yourselves, y'heah?" and they said, "Yes, sir. Take care of yourself, sir."

Out of earshot down the road, Buford said, "Goin' where, Roan? Where were you and papa goin'?"

"No place." Roan shook his head. "Just talking, earlier. About—after"—he gestured vaguely to the night.

"Been at Staunton a few days," Buford said. "Drilling and such. Tonight was the first chance I got to ask a pass. Funny, Roan, we should have picked the same night. Makes a man believe strange things—like thinking goin' across space the way telegraphing goes down a wire. We've been like that a lot, in our time." He turned his face toward his brother. "Ever notice?"

"Yes." Roan's throat hurt. "Yes. I have." *Let go m'brother! I do his fighting for him till he grows.*

"Roan," Buford said. "I'm awful proud of you. I couldn't say that to any other living man the way I mean it. Kind of makes me feel inside like you was a girl I wanted to kiss," he laughed. "I ain't agoin' to kiss you, so don't draw back, but I'm awful proud of you, boy. A sergeant of Ashby's Cav'ry! Boy!"

"That's good, huh?" Roan smiled.

"Damn good, for my money." Buford nodded once or twice. Then he said, "I'm turnin' off just beyond, Roan. The road down toward Waller's Creek that follows the railroad in to town. Could I ask you something?" His voice was solemn soft. For a moment Roan couldn't draw his breath and his heart was white cold within him. *Dear God,* he thought, *don't let the finger be upon Buford like it was on Forney Manigault when he saw death at Manassas. Don't let Buford tell me that he sees it grinning at him now. Don't God, don't.*

"Go ahead, Bufe, ask."

"Well," Buford said, "what's it like? Just that, I reckon. What's it like, Roan?"

The reprieve in Roan was like a live thing, leaping for joy. It pressed his throat tight so that he could not talk. But he could breathe again and think again, and with the thinking came the hopeless, futile knowledge that no man who's been in it can ever really tell it right. There are no words.

"How do you mean, Bufe?"

"Well," Bufe said thoughtfully, "just that, I reckon. Just what's it like in a battle? I never thought one way or another to fight a man with fists. If he was big, I reckon I fought harder 'cause I was scared. Reckon I never thought if I was brave or a coward. But I'd kind of like to know what it's like—if you can tell me?"

Roan's impulse was to fling his arm tightly across Bufe's shoulders to hold him close, but it was too late for that. Too late now for everything. *I can't do his fighting for him any longer, for he's grown.* With that he laughed, and the sound was horrid against the silence of the night. "That's all it is, Bufe, boy. Just what you said. If he's big, you just fight harder, 'cause yo're scared!" Then Roan did put his hand on Buford's shoulder, not his arm around, but his hand tight, fingers pressing hard. The anger in the paddock was gone from his soul with the faint and distant echo of the past. "I reckon yo're grown, Bufe. Take care of yoreself, y'hear?"

"You, too, Roan. Here's m'turn-off. Good luck."

Roan threw his leg over Lady and sat for a moment looking down at his younger brother, getting the boy's face full in mind as he saw it now. And his heart was quiet within him, for he knew now that, win or lose, you never throw the cards in, for the money never buys anyway—beyond the satisfaction of your own soul for the playing.

Buford stood there in the roadway, his face turned to the sound of the scrabbling hoofbeats, his mouth open still to call good-by once again, but it was too far now for Roan to hear. So, after a moment, he turned his back and put his tired boy's legs into the last ten miles back into Staunton, to the job in hand.

It was lightening for dawn by the time Roan worked his way up into the high country where he'd left his patrol. "All hell's breaking open soon," they told him. "Word's been coming all the way down the line all night. Frémont's man Milroy has got thirty-seven hundred Yankees in McDowell Village, foot of Bull Pasture Mountain right ahead of us, with a regiment deployed on Shenandoah Mountain. Rest of Frémont's army is strung along South Branch Valley. Schenk's Brigade is thirty-four miles north at Franklin, and Frémont himself is still in Petersburg, with Blenker's Division not yet quit of Romney! That's seventy-five miles of stringing out, sarge. There's goin' to be some fancy clobberin' heahabouts before day is done!"

"What with—four cav'ry troops?"

"Hell. Ain't y'heard? Jackson's back!"

Roan was too far upcountry to see. But Buford, jogging fast into Staunton to make reveille, saw.

When the first train rolled slowly into Staunton Station, folks didn't know what for, beyond just a train. Then somebody recognized Clubby Johnson forming up the companies, with his big stick to hand instead of a sword—shouting in that loud voice of his he didn't even soften to say sweet words to the ladies. By that time the next train close behind was clanking to a steam-spitting stop and the third-brigade regiments began piling off—the 10th, 23rd and 37th Virginia—taking it on the double to clear the tracks, forming column in the street beside. "Stonewall's back!" The word smoked through town like brush fire in a quick wind shift and folks came arunning leaving lay what be—death, childbirth and taxes. Down to the depot to see it and breathe it and shout inside with the joy of it.

"Damn if Stonewall didn't march us clean to Mechum's Station, without a word of whereto! Cars come in and marshaled and ev'one swore to hell we're headed for Richmond. Trains were all set to pull—and they pulled. But west and back again—not east! And by Garry for breakfast, heah we are, to git that bastoon Frémont!" More trains were pulling, as far down the single track as you could see. Stopping and letting off. First brigade now—the "Stonewall" since Manassas, under that fancy General Winder—2nd, 4th, 5th, 27th and 33rd Virginia, piling down and forming columns.

"What for y'ask? I'll tell you what for! That Tom Jackson's plenty smart, in spite of what some say. Ev'body in the Valley thought he'd snuck out—so did Banks and so did Frémont! That's why Jackson done it—to make them believe! Between the two, the Yankees've got forty thousand men, once they jine up. But they ain't agoin' to jine now. Stonewall kept Ashby wedged between, and now he's all between himself with six thousand men to put the clobber on one and one, piecemeal, before they know which side's painted. Hold up theah! Wait for pappy!"

You could see General Jackson then through the troops forming in the streets and the troops detraining. Here a minute for a
quick sight of him putting a word to Captain Hotchkiss. Gone
then, walking slow and thoughtful, and there again bending an
ear to General Winder's question. Not a smidgin of haste in him,
nor excitement, with the crowds cheering him and the little boys
yelling shrill. Just tall and calm and quiet, with his beard combed
out with morning and his eyes so blue it hurt to look into them.
His old overcoat buttoned tight for a while, then draped to his
arm as the heat of the day came full. Once in a while, thumb and
finger to his cap visor where it was burred, to pull it down firm.
Seeing all of it, prodding hard for it to be the way he wanted,
oblivious to whatever else but what he had to do—but powerful
thankful in his soul that this fight wasn't coming up for Sunday.
Stonewall's back!

Upcountry twenty-two miles, the cavalry dismounted to
fight on foot. Sent the horses back with horse holders and took
the line with carbines to pin the flung-out Yankee pickets.
Pinned 'em cold until Old Clubby Ed Johnson came double-
quicking his advance-guard march up to take over. Took over
and went through, waving his big hickory club like a drum major
and shouting blue billy for bumblebees. Yanks recognized him.
"There's old Johnson! Let's flank him!" and Clubby yelled back,
"Yes, damn you! Flank me if you can!" and he drove on through
the regiment on the mountain, developing the fight around
McDowell Village.

It was a rifle fight, Bull Pasture, when the third brigade came
up, laid on across jagged, sawtoothed mountains where a cat
could hardly cling, let alone wheeled artillery. Four hours of lead
drenching, with the barrels hot to frying eggs, and both sides
scrambling the steep slopes for position and neither getting it too
well. Roan's troop was in part of it, dismounted, when it began
to break toward nightfall. Not long, but just enough for him to
know he wasn't waiting for it any longer. His flesh was cool in

sweat with the mountain winds, but there was no faint quiver of expectation left in it. Firm and hard and slow-triggered.

Then darkness came down and the Yanks in the village began to pull out, heading for the bridge, retiring under cover of what artillery they could bring to bear on the flat. Pulled out about a mile and built a lot of campfires—and pulled out again, leaving the fires to cover for them while they headed north for Franklin, telescoping the whole of Frémont's army back on itself and making sure, for all bets, that there wouldn't be no junction with Banks yet awhile!

Roan found Buford with his jacket off, digging trenches to bury Yankee dead. Whole Institute Corps was burying—to harden the boys up, some said. But the hell with that—Jackson himself had let 'em march upcountry with his own old Stonewall Brigade—and that's enough for a start in war, for any man's money.

"H'are y', Bufe."

"Hello, Roan." Buford sleeved the sweat off his face and came up grinning, shovel in hand. "Some fight, I reckon, by the sound. Didn't get to see much with," he said distinctly, "the Stonewall Brigade held in reserve."

Roan grunted. "Never do see much. Jest what's around you."

"Sure," Buford nodded. "So I reckon we'll go back to Lexington now, what with exams six weeks ahead, and not even see that much."

"I reckon," Roan said.

"But I'll be back," Buford said, and he wagged his head emphatically, "because it ain't no more than just what you said— 'if he's big, you fight harder, 'cause you're scared!' "

The bodies weren't covered. They lay beside the lengthening trench just as they had been littered in, with the earthy smell of death rising from them like swamp mist. Too many of them to give personality back to any. Ohio boys from the Maumee— Western Virginia boys from the coal country. Dead soldiers left behind forever in the backwash of a lost fight, with dirty hands and wrenched faces softening to peace in the quiet nobility that comes upon those who die under God's sky to go down into God's earth as they lie—with no tribal trappings of funeral pomp and circumstance to make them seem asleep—no paint and flowers and music to give the lie to Death.

"It's a little more," Roan said softly. "I couldn't tell you when you asked, for it wasn't in me then, but it is now, Bufe."

"What, Roan?"

Roan looked at his brother closely. "Bufe," he said, "life takes a lot of living, but only one dying. I don't know how it happened"—he shook his head—"but I died a little bit over at Mossy Creek the other day, so now, when it really comes, I've got it all to do over again." He smiled. "Will you remember that, Bufe—if you come back—just don't—die too many times. Bufe, I'm hungry. Let's eat."

Jackson's operation against Frémont's advanced forces west of the Shenandoah Mountains rolled Milroy back onto Schenk at Franklin Village and precluded any immediate possibility of Frémont's joining Banks through the gaps west of Staunton. Banks, in the maneuver, had been completely hoodwinked by Jackson and almost literally "marched around." A sensitive Banks might have conceived the idea that he had been ignored. But Banks was not at all sensitive, merely cautious, so like Montgomery pivoting on Rheims, he withdrew from Harrisonburg and shuttled north up the Valley to New Market. To his superiors in Washington, he was merely shortening his lines. To himself he thought he was giving Jackson no opportunity to make a lightning move on him. If Jackson so intended, Banks, the political strategist turned soldier, would throw him off balance and out of timing.

Clever Banks! Because immediately he knew he had hoodwinked Jackson. He knew he had hoodwinked Jackson because Jackson's man Ashby put cavalry pressure on him immediately both frontally and from the westward—and cavalry pressure is the setup for an attack. So Banks withdrew to consolidate for that attack, knowing full well that by moving first he had brought Jackson beyond the break of measure and thus precluded surprise.

Had a frontal attack on Banks been Jackson's next plan, Banks would have been dead right. But it was not. Jackson was in no position, on his manpower factor alone, to assault at odds better than two to one against him. He could not reduce Banks with the battle axe, but he could slit his throat with the military scalpel. And he did.

When Banks' rear guard under Ashby's pressure cleared the east-west road that crosses the Valley Turnpike at right angles through New Market, Jackson began to force the northern march of his main body. Banks was telescoping rapidly for the twenty-five miles to Strasburg—canalized between the long run of Little North Mountain to the west and the Massanutton range to the east.

Now a jug'll make the old men see it all again, when thunder growls in the Massanuttons, for the glory of it will hang on the high crags forever. Best keep off those mountains when the mists coil thick—or once again they'll come marching. Old rooster-necked Dick Ewell, with his stomach growling loud on the frumenty he fed himself for mortal fear of gut-rot. The First Brigade they always called the "Stonewall" since Manassas. Frying pans stuck down their rifle barrels. The singing Louisiana Boys in white gaiters; dancing like women at night, without a straggler on the day's long march; fighting to the sound of the guns like the Devil gone corn-juice happy. With Old Jack everywhere the line along. Telling nothing, giving no word. Camping his regiments at crossroads so they could talk at night but never guess which road for dawn, until the march started. And then, by Cracky, *reaching New Market* and *turning sharp east for the Massanuttons. Close enough to smell the wind in Banks' tail feathers—and walking away from it! Who's crazy now? Tom Fool Jackson they said—all but his own men. His men just kept on marching.*

Up and up and up into the mist-hung mountain forests. Leaving Banks behind. Climbing over and down across South Fork to Luray. Then turning north in Page Valley. Now it came plain even to the lumberheads. He's marching around Banks again, but this time to get Banks himself. He's paralleling Banks' army, with the Massanuttons to screen his move and when he comes out at Front Royal he'll be across Banks' supply lines!

So press it, Brother! Beat yore feet. Richmond's tottering behind you with McClellan beating on the door. But she ain't fell yet! Jackson's three-o'clock-in-the-morning-men, marching before dawn except when Old Blue Light starts the night before. And don't ask questions, Gawd A'Mighty—for there he is, ridin' Old

Sorrel, heavin' his own tired shoulder to a bogged-down gun, mud in his beard, caked hard.

Banks slept at Strasburg, behind his trenches. You can't fool Senator Banks. Jackson is way down south. This is only Ashby's scouts knocking on the door and I'll so notify Washington tomorrow. No, Siree. Only you can't fool with God either. If God intends a man to be a senator, Abe Lincoln himself best not try to make him a major general!

Jackson came out of his valley at Front Royal across the Manassas Gap Flail Road—Banks' direct line of communications with Washington. Part of the breach of the Front Royal lines was the Confederate cavalry charge in column of fours at the gallop on the Winchester Road. Banks got out of the pocket by taking one side of the triangle into Winchester while Jackson fought down the longer hypothenuse. But Banks left his supplies almost intact—shoes and blankets, food and medicines, ammunition, tentage, and wagons. Mr. Commissary Banks to Jackson's men thereafter.

There was a time when Jackson personally fought his advance guard through the dark streets of Winchester—returning, as he had promised little Molly Lentaigne. The impetus of attack drove the victorious Valley Army on north until once more they saw the Potomac and frightened Washington.

But only briefly, for the price of giving Banks a tactics lesson, was time again. And time was allowing Frémont the opportunity to close from the west behind Jackson, almost to join Shields, closing from the east.

So Jackson slipped back through the closing door at Strasburg—actually through the extreme range fire of Shields' and Frémont's advance guards—and retreated once more to fight the slow pursuit again at Cross Keys and Port Republic, by which time the focus of battle had shifted to Richmond.

Let there be no doubt that part of McClellan's failure in the Seven Days' Battle was the fact that Jackson's Valley defeat of Frémont and Banks, piecemeal, and his outsmarting of Shields, so *frightened Washington that McClellan again could not count on the vast power play of troops he thought he had to crush Richmond.*

But then again there was another ingredient that thwarted McClellan, that he did not dream of. Jackson slipped out of the Valley stalemate, moving swiftly in the dark cloak of complete secrecy, and struck McClellan's north-right flank and rolled him up like a rug—to the James River!

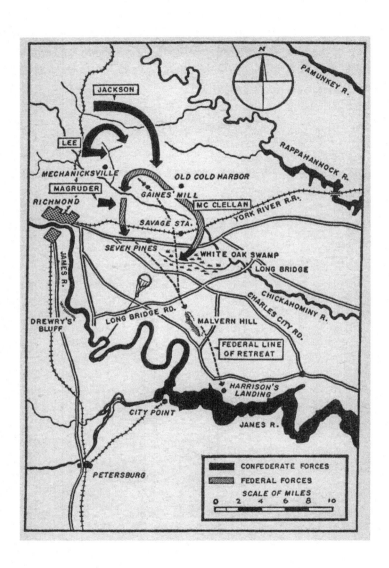

THE SECRET OF
THE SEVEN DAYS

THE TENSION EASED up a bit after the Cross Keys and Port Republic fights. Up in the Shenandoah Valley, on June eighth, Stonewall Jackson met Frémont's Fed Army at Cross Keys and drove him back on Harrisonburg—losing poor, gallant Turner Ashby. The next day Jackson crossed the river at Port Republic and drove General Shields' army back up the Luray Valley. Three days later, down Richmond way, Gen. J.E.B. Stuart—the same who was a lieutenant colonel up at Manassas the year before— rode his twelve hundred cavalry thundering around McClellan's hundred and five thousand 'sieging army—from Mechanicsville on the north clear almost to the James River on the south—to show up the whole Yankee threat for a loose-jointed heavy hand over Richmond with scant power to close the fist, now that Robert Edward Lee was in command.

That was when Davin Ancrum got the letter from his father that if he got anywhere near his Great-Aunt Honor Summerhayes' place, he was to drop by for another horse to replace the one he had to shoot. So Davin showed the letter and got a three-day pass to go down Charlottesville way to Aunt Honor's horse farm.

Roan Catlett grinned, "Slack times a three-day pass is good for two weeks, but you come back, y'hear? With Forney Manigault out for wounds, I don't aim to git ridin' orders, without you with me for luck, boy!"

"Well"—Davin waved his pass—"if anything starts, Gin'ral Jackson'll know where to find me. Just tell him to come git me."

It was a bright June day when Davin crossed the Blue Ridge, with heavy heat to come, by the fast way the mists smoked off the treetops after sunrise. He felt free and light in spirit. His own man, for sure. Turned full sixteen with this past year of Valley fighting, but with boy still hiding under it. Funny how that could be. Like two people, almost.

Davin laughed at both. "I sure'n hell ain't still goin' to school studying books—whatever else!"

He caught a mule ride halfway up Brown's Gap and a couple of rides in army wagons farther along. A great golden day, getting better to live in, each mile east. A day to slowly meet a yellow-haired girl in a pale blue dress, with a silver ribbon to her hair.

Davin met a hearse. Caught up with it rather, a few miles beyond Mechum's River Station. A real old-fashioned hearse with glass sides where they weren't busted out, and lacquered urns and white feather plumes on it, moth-eaten somewhat—like the old white-muzzled jug-heads that pulled it. Old Negra on the box; beside him a quartermaster captain in a brand-new uniform frock coat and sword, his arm in a black silk sling. Two soldiers stood below in the road, spitting and waiting like soldiers do, for the next word of what happens.

The captain turned slowly on the box and looked down at Davin walking along. "About time you showed up, trooper. Just follow along…. Come on, Neb; tickle 'em up," and the hearse started off again down the dirt road.

Davin looked at the two dusty soldiers. They were about the same height and in the same state of campaign shabbiness that he was. An infantryman and an artilleryman.

The beetle-crusher held out his hand. "Threewhitts m'name, scout. Thirty-Third Virginians. 'Lousy' Thirty-Third—but we git to git a bath and spankin' new uniforms, soon's we reach Richmond."

"That so?" Davin said. "Well, I had a bath yesterday, and I don't aim t'go t'Richmond."

"Talk yoreself out of Christmas, wouldn't y', bub? Suppose t'be four of us for funeral escort—infantry, artillery, cav'ry, and we pick up the quartermaster up in Richmond, where they got plenty of them lyin' aroun' loose."

Davin shook his head. "I'm out of Gin'ral Turner Ashby's lot. I got a three-day pass for down Charlottesville way. That's where I'm goin'."

"Hell," Threewhitts winked, "you wouldn't up and spoil a man's fine funeral, now would you, scout?"

"What's it got to do with me?" Davin said. "I got a legal pass."

"Sure, sure," Threewhitts said. "Only Captain Scott Barnaby here'll write you an extension. Got too much other trouble to let you go, now he's got you. Body ain't fresh's it might be. Buried for a time after it happened. Brought an undertaker up from Richmond, but you know how it is, the weather turns warm. Sealed iron casket with a window in it. But the family wants burial in Richmond and the captain's got plenty money on him to see it happens that way. Know any girls in Richmond?"

"Only my Cousin Tandy," Davin said, "but I still ain't agoin'."

The artilleryman jerked his head toward the casket in the hearse. "Brigadier General Chadwick McHoes," he said. "Acting Deputy Quartermaster General of all of Jeff Davis' armies. His hoss blew up on him. M'name's Tom Jourdin. The Revrund Doctor Captain Pendleton's old batt'ry. Just got over wounds."

"His hoss blew up?"

Jourdin said, "Sure'n hell hit did. Shell went right inside the animule. Blew up inside. Wasn't any hoss left and precious little general, they tell."

With that, the three of them walked on silently for a while, trailing the old mule-drawn hearse.

"They got observation balloons for the fightin' down around Richmond," Threewhitts said presently. "I sure aim to see 'em if I can. Read in the papers how. Yanks call theirs the Intrepid. They got a balloon professor who ascends it up with a wire down from it—from over the Chickahominy near Gaines' Mill—to look-see our lines and tell back by telegraph. Got to git up a thousand feet to stay clear of our Whitworth guns south of the river."

"Yo're plumb crazy," Jourdin said. "A thousand feet is way the hell high an' up!"

"We got any?" Davin asked.

"Sort of a one," Threewhits nodded. "Homemade like. We gas it up in Richmond tied to an engine and run it up and down the York River Rail Road to ascend it up our side of the fighting, paper says."

"That's somethin', I reckon," Davin said. "Saw one go up once. Market Fair at Staunton befoh the wah. Fellow hanging on it too. Striped tights."

Wasn't any use arguing this escort thing. Just walk along with it for company and beggar off casually when he got to Aunt Honor's. The only thing was that walking and talking to the two others, the whole escort pulled in under Aunt Honor's side portico and stopped before Davin quite realized where he was.

Aunt Honor Summerhayes was a fixture. Summerhayeses are old people around Charlottesville, and old people tend to breed up fixtures. It won't do her kindly to tell how she looked, but you should see how, to understand. A big woman. Big to tall, that is. Not through. Through, she was no thicker than a thin strong man'd be, any place. Only one better horseman in the whole Commonwealth of Virginia than Miz Honor. Jeb Stuart. Bred horses, Miz Honor. Years of it made her look sort of like a horse, like married people get to look alike. But powerful kind to her people. A great hand for charity. Took care of all the poor people miles around—even if it killed them.

"Well, Scott," she said to the captain, "I got your lettah, but you took long enough getting here! Put the hearse out in the barn for the night and come in for suppah. What are these soldiers doing with you?"

"Escort, ma'am."

"Not that boy there." Aunt Honor pointed a bony finger at Davin. "That boy's an Ancrum." She looked Davin questioningly in the eye for a moment. "Can't call your name, son," she said, "but you've got Ancrum blood. Not the Dinwaldie Ancrums, I'd say. A hand or so higher than the Dinwaldies, and broader in the withers. I reckon the senator's line. Over Short Mountain way?"

"That's right, ma'am. M'father wrote I was t'git a hoss."

"For sure!" Aunt Honor boomed. "Come in, y'all!"

The captain looked at the hearse. "In the barn, you said, ma'am?"

"Where else?" Aunt Honor squinted at him hard. "I've known Chad McHoes since I wore pigtails. He's all packed and loaded, so there's no need unloading—with all the fuss of flowers and charcoal saucers. Besides, it's bad luck—when you're not buryin' from the house. Never liked Chad too much anyway. It's his brother Beckwith I'm doing this fer."

After supper, Aunt Honor took Davin into the house office.

"Lucky you're goin' to Richmond," she said. "You can take Cousin Tandy's silk wedding dress down. I'll wrap it for you, dampproof. I've got a three-year-old hunter for you, son. Eclipse blood with a strong strain of Bright-eyes too. Been hidin' him from the commandeering——"

"But I'm not——Eclipse blood? C'n I see him, Aunt Honor!"

"The family was at the Spotswood Hotel for a while," Aunt Honor said, "but they've opened the old house again—on Broad Street back of the Governor's Mansion."

"But, ma'am, I'm not——"

"Opened it for Cousin Tandy's wedding. Not rightly theirs, the house. Inherited it from the Linthicums when Uncle Sloane married Miss Sarah Linthicum. She died of child fever. Cousin Tandy's Wade's daughter. Summer-hayes, that is. Drinks too much—and rides a hoss like a hill Negra—Wade, that is. Married Thalia Ancrum from Dinwaldie. Thin girl. Vaporish."

"But, Aunt Honor, this Captain Barnaby has made a mis——"

"Wedding dress is a tradition. Belonged to the Duchesse de Saussure, one of Louis Philippe's never-mind. When Grandfather Cassals was Secretary of Legation he married her, back in the 'Thirties. Then Cousin Chastity wore it when she married that schoolteaching popinjay who died of a consumption in Natchez."

"I'm trying to tell you, ma'am——"

"Next it went over to your branch when your sister, Henrietta, married Brainerd Manigault. Brainerd got killed the other day, they tell me. Well, Henrietta'll get someone else, with her roving eye, you mark. Your father sent the dress down here to me— to get it to Richmond somehow. I reckon you're the somehow. Senator puts great store on family tradition. Great store."

"M'father?" Davin said. "He wants it down? Well—I——"

They loaded the great iron casket on a flatcar down at Charlottesville Station the next day and rigged a tent fly over it for shade. Captain Barnaby paid off the hearse and got blankets for the escort.

The Virginia Central Rail Road ran pretty close to the Yankee right wing on the north, after it left Noel's Junction heading for Richmond, but they had jump tracks up there to route cars down the Richmond, Fredericksburg and Potomac line. The flatcar with the casket got side-tracked off for supply trains a couple of times. The three of them settled to it in soldier boredom, getting food now and then at the stops. Second morning, when Davin pulled the blankets off his face, where he was lying with the bundle of Cousin Tandy's wedding dress for a pillow, the car was on a siding and stopped. He could smell city all around—damp stone pavements and the dusty spice smell of horse drays, cindery smoke and the dry breath of pine packing cases.

It was just coming light. Jourdin was sitting on the casket, scratching his armpit inside his shirt, getting ready to pull his boots on.

"Cap'n Barnaby woke me awhile back," he said. "He's gone up to town to arrange. Got to get the quartermaster fella to make four for escort, and borry a gun caisson from some defense batt'ry."

Threewhitts yawned and sat up. Davin rolled the blankets and looped the bundle of Cousin Tandy's wedding dress across his shoulders with the rope he'd rigged.

"Left half an hour ago, walking," Jourdin said. "Funeral's supposed to be from St. Paul's Church, but we got first to tote him up and leave him lay in state at the Capitol near Eleventh all day for folks t'see. Then the captain's got to get new uniforms for us. He's walkin'. Be a right smart time he's gone, I reckon."

Threewhitts looked around slowly, taking his bearings. "This yere must be Fourteenth Street leading over Mayo's Bridge, with the Richmond docks the other side. Y'all smell bacon cookin'?" Threewhitts drew a deep breath. "Damn if I don't!" He pointed. "Down by the bridge"—and he scrambled fast off the car.

"Can't all go," Davin shook his head. "Somebody's got to stay with the general."

Threewhitts looked at Jourdin. "How then? Match? Two to go first and scout it up for breakfast, then spell the other one to go?"

Davin and Threewhitts walked across the tracks and climbed up the bank to Fourteenth Street where it leads onto the bridge. The other side, below, the bridge-guard relief was cooking in a skillet around a little scrap-wood fire. They spoke them and made a deal on account of being out of Ashby's Cavalry and the 33rd Virginians of the Stonewall Brigade. "That so? Well, sure 'nuff. Long way from home, ain't you? Gather 'round."

With his mouth full, sitting on the bridge bank, Davin saw the little steamboat tied up on the far side of the wharves beyond the bridge. Great bubble of bright-colored rags heaped beside it on the dock. Like to smother the steamboat under, if it fell over on it. Like to fall over on it any minute too; because the rag clutter was ruffling up high like something was trying to get out from under—swelling like a great multicolored blister—ballooning.

Davin choked. "There she is, Threewhitts!"

"She's just that freakin' balloon," the guard corporal snorted. "They gassing it up from the dock main. Don't any of them know how to work it, you ask me. Blow th'selves up someday sure."

"What about Tom Jourdin's breakfast?"

"Match you." Davin flipped a coin.

Davin walked down to the dock. They had this thing hooked up to a wheel gas valve beside the mooring, filling it full with a powerful hosing sound and a stench of raw gas you could have hung a blanket roll on. A pile of mismatched silk like a patchwork quilt. The crew on the dock were walking out the great silk folds, keeping them smooth for filling, spreading the rolled part flat and keeping the basket ropes clear from snarling the fishnet that went around the outside.

The sergeant fella with them had a twisted leg that bent outward at the knee, instead of front and back. Quite a trick for him to walk with it, so he stood mostly, shouting how.

"Howdy, bub." He looked at Davin. "Never saw one of these yere contraptions before, I reckon?"

"Yes, I did," Davin said. "Up at Staunton Market Fair three years ago, I saw one."

"Saw me, then"—the sergeant nodded. "Made m'living at it. Ascented up at Staunton, three years ago."

"Striped tights?" Davin asked.

"Striped tights," the sergeant nodded solemnly. "The Miraculous Wizard Watts, Professor of Applied Aeronautics."

"That's something!" Davin said. "You goin' up now?"

"Nope." Watts shook his head. "Busted m'leg at Philadelphia right after Staunton," and he pointed at his knee, flexing it so Davin could see how it worked. "Besides, they got a cav'ry lieutenant fer that—who can draw on the map what he sees. Lieutenant Barraclough."

Davin nodded. "Balloon at Staunton was all one color—silver. How comes it this one's like a rainbow?"

Wade snorted. "This yere's a project. When they got the idea we had to have a balloon to match the Yanks, they don't have silk to make one. What'd they do? Collected ev'ry silk dress from ev'ry girl fer miles around! Made a man feel mighty indecent to be around it until the gas killed the perfume smell." Watts winked. "Boudoir nervous. Come on, lay off your blanket bundle and give us a hand here"—and he bent quickly to the snarling net ropes, feeding them back to Davin to lay clear.

"It ain't m'blanket bundle. It's my Cousin Tandy's wedding"—and then with sudden mountain shrewdness—"present," he said, and snugged the end of the bundle tight under his arm. "Well," he said, "I reckon I better mosey."

Sergeant Watts straightened up. "Say, wait a minute." Davin gripped the bundle tighter. "Where you from? You ain't a Richmond soljer."

"Ashby's Cav'ry, up in the Valley. Leastwise Ashby's, until he got killed. Don't know whose now."

"It's true then, ain't it?" Watts fixed him with an intent eye. "About General Jackson being in Richmond last night, conferencing with General Lee?"

"I—don't know. Just got in t'day m'self. Gin'ral Jackson was bivouacked at Madison's Cove up in the Valley when I left three days ago. How could he be here?"

"You're here, ain't you?" Watts pursed his lips. "So could Jackson be. He moves around, they tell," and he laughed. "You ain't lyin'?"

Davin shook his head, but there was a vague unrest upon him suddenly. It didn't set right now, to be so far away from his outfit. Out of hand of news from people he knew, and things he had learned to feel instinctively for true or false. The lost-dog feeling of soldiers on their own.

"They goin' up soon's it's full?" he asked awkwardly.

"That's why I asked you. We been ascending before by running her down the York River Rail Road on an engine. Now we got these orders to hook her up to this yere steamboat and run her down the James."

"That so? What's down the James to look at? McClellan's army's up the north between Mechanicsville and White Oak Swamp."

"That's just it. Ain't nothin' down the James. Yankee gunboats near Bermuda Hundred and transports at City Point is all."

"What then?"

"Well"—Watts winked—"if I was a Yank and seen this balloon go up down the James to look-see, I'd get itchy about what for. It'd draw my attention why it ain't up North side around the Chickahominy where it always was before. Wouldn't it you? Like mebbe we want 'em to think we're gettin' set to hit 'em down the James River side."

"So they pull a lot of reserves down to prepare against it. That yore idea?"

Sergeant Watts shrugged. "Why not? If Stonewall Jackson was in Richmond last night, his Valley army may be right behind. He hits the Feds north in the Mechanicsville flank and keeps 'em movin' toward the James till they're rolled clean up on themselves, right to left, like a parlor rug, come spring cleaning!"

The unease in Davin stirred again. He turned and looked back the way he had come. Threewhitts and Jourdin were nowhere in sight. There was some distant artillery firing up to the north, but not hot. Just then half a dozen folds each side of the main balloon bubble caught the gas full, and rippled into the rising mass of silk, swelling it high above them, with the rope net snarling again under their feet so they had to jump clear.

There was this Lieutenant Barraclough yelling now for everybody to give a hand, and Davin grabbed hold with the rest of the crew. They drew the covering net clear of its tangle and rove out the shrouds of basket ropes, walking them down aboard the steamboat to where the basket lay on the afterdeck beside the anchor-rope winch. You could feel the silk bag begin to tug now. Lot of force in the gas and coming in fast.

"Get up topside, some of you fellas!" Watts yelled. "Fend her clear the funnel befoh a spark catches her!" With somebody on shore screaming, "Fend her off the trees!" and everybody running around, some on the lower deck with axes cutting the mooring ropes and the man at the gas valve turning the wheel frantically, like a brakeman on a runaway steam car.

The balloon made a noise inside like a great drum booming once, muffled, and it swelled suddenly full round, drawing the net snug and jerking the shroud lines taut. The basket, on its side on the deck, jerked up to sit on its bottom, spewing out sandbags and glasses and a map board. Then the man at the valve snaffled the gas neck tight with a strap and unhooked it free of the pipe. With that the bag leaped straight up aft of the steamer to the limit of the anchor rope, carrying the basket with it until the bottom of it was four feet above the deck with the snubbed anchor rope drumming like a bull-fiddle string—and the steamer in midstream, its engine throbbing.

A cut of panic knifed through Davin at sight of the water between him and shore, but like all things in the army you can't do anthing about, it left nothing but the determination that they still wouldn't get Cousin Tandy's wedding dress to put with the extras in the patch bin forward, against rips and tears. Absent without leave you could talk away or take the punishment, but this wedding dress his father——

They had the sandbags gathered together to rerig on the basket rim and Lieutenant Barraclough stood with the map board and glasses while half a dozen men tried to wind down the winch to bring the basket back to deck. They were coming around the bend now, with the navy yard left, heading south down the James toward Drewry's Bluff. Davin couldn't just stand there, so he turned to help, building up credit for himself against a letdown, which was his usual way. Winch would let out, but they couldn't get it to grind down.

"Give somebody a leg up!" Watts yelled. "Then hand him the sandbags; that'll weight it!"

A dozen of them had their hands up, clawing at the basket, Davin with them. They looked at one another and one made a hand stirrup. "Come on, son," and before Davin really knew he was doing it, he put his foot in and they hoicked him high enough to grab the basket rim and tumble headfirst inside. When he got his head over, they began to pass up the sandbags.

Lieutenant Barraclough handed up the map board and field glasses. "There're racks for them," he said, and just as he said it, the winch ratchet let go in a running metallic shriek and the basket shot thirty feet up and stuck again.

It knocked Davin flat inside and took the breath out of him. When he got his head over the rim that time, the thirty feet was not only up but it was aft as well, over the steamer's muddy wake.

Lieutenant Barraclough stood in the stern, shouting at him through cupped hands, "Sit tight! Don't try to slide down the rope!"

Then for half an hour they worked on the winch, sweating and hammering and cursing it, while Davin watched them, and the steamboat plowed on toward Drewry's Bluff.

The lieutenant kept calling to him off and on. Finally he said, "Look, trooper. We can't grind you down, and if you slide down the rope, I can't get up to observe. We can head back in and call it off or we can let you up farther, for you to do the observing. Which'll it be?"

"Well, I don't know, sir I ain't never——"

"That toggle to the hoop above you is the rip cord. If you go all the way up, you can pull that to let the gas out and bring you down. Coming down, if it's too fast, you dump out sand."

"Yes, I know—but——"

"All you do is look for dust on the roads to indicate troop movement," Barraclough shouted, "and mark the map! It's the Gilmer map. Nine sixteenths of an inch to the mile. You're a cavalryman. It's just like horse scouting, only from higher up!"

"How—far—up—is higher up?" Davin shouted.

"That's Drewry's Bluff ahead, left." Barraclough pointed. "High enough only for you to see well over north and as far east as City Point. Higher if they shoot!"

"Higher if they—what?"

And just then the ratchet began to hammer shrill again, the men at the winch leaped back, shouting, and the balloon bounded upward with a jerk that knocked Davin flat again and a rush of air that gagged him. When he finally got his head over the rim that time, the steamboat was a tiny toy way below and the whole James River no wider than a farm ditch. His face frozen in fear, he hung on for a few minutes, his eyes tight shut, pulling up on the basket rim. The basket was turning slowly as the gasbag turned, but after a few minutes it came steady and he opened his eyes, and suddenly it was the most amazing thing in the whole wide world, and the pure exhilaration of it drenched his soul in awful beauty.

He could see way east and north now—miles, when he used the field glasses.

Must be fourteen miles to the Yankee right wing at Mechanicsville Bridge. Couldn't get to make that out for sure, but he could sure enough see the Chickahominy and White Oak Swamp six or seven miles northeast, where McClellan had his left wing secured. Then suddenly in the high silence, he heard distant artillery fire. He put the glasses north to try to see the red of shell bursts in the haze, but it was still too far. Up Mechanicsville way. "By glory, mebbe Stonewall Jackson has sneaked down to help jasperoo them, and I'm missing it!"

He came in closer with the glasses and caught a line of light blue ammunition wagons raising a long plume of dust toward where the Long Bridge Road joins with Willis Church. Marked them down on the map. Over east between Crenshaw's and where Western Run crosses, there was a column of infantry marching north. Low dust, thick-clouded. Two regiments anyway, by the column length—moving toward the gunfire. He marked them down. Then it got so easy it made him chuckle. Just like hossback scouting, except you could see everything. Cavalry moving north out of W. M. Harrison's Landing—high dust and thin, and four artillery batteries turning left at the sawmill near Mt. Prospect.

He was so excited he shouted down what he was seeing, even though it was way too far to hear. He could see the steamboat, tiny as a water bug, well south of Drewry's Bluff now, with the rippled wake out back and the bow wave front, like swimming legs. He went back to his work, spotting more dust moving north on the roads, all the while the artillery fire way up there got hotter and heavier, like the long roll on distant drums. "Sure'n hell there's a big battle making! It must be Gin'ral Jackson's come down from the Valley! It must be—and I'm missing it!"

That time, when he looked down at the steamboat, there was no wake or bow wave to her and she was canted around sideways to the river current, tipped slightly to her port side with the tug of the balloon rope on her stern. Grounded hard on a sand bar. The rope trailed east straight across the river and the Yankee side of the bank, with the wind that pressured the bag. Smoke puffs there were, from the riverbank, like rifle fire and, by Garry, it was rifle fire—with a platoon of blue coats scrambling down the banks to get closer range on the steamer. The wind caught the bag hard now and tugged the anchor rope almost straight, carrying the basket over farther inland. They'd sure enough capture the steamboat, caught as she was on the bar; then they'd capture him. No blessed fear, they'd capture him!

For a white moment of panic, he tried to remember exactly what the lieutenant had told him. Let sand out to go higher; pull the rip cord to come down. He pulled Cousin Tandy's wedding-dress bundle tighter around his shoulder, clutched the map board and pulled on the rip cord. Nothing happened for a moment, except the basket seemed to drift farther inland on the anchor rope. Drifting, it brought the ground closer up to him. He pulled harder and, looking back, found he could no longer see the river, only little blue figures running from it. There were trees coming up fast toward him now, so he pulled a few sandbag dump cords. That slowed the trees, but not too much, for a moment later he could see the leaves on them. Then the anchor rope was slicing into them, snipping leaves in a green cloud behind. Then the basket plowed into top branches and the great silk bubble went on ahead and settled, rippling out flat like a great spread crazy quilt.

Davin got out fast, fell a bit, and began to climb down. He could hear distant shouting from the direction of the James, and a few scattered rifle shots; so he headed off in the opposite direction, going fast toward the north by the sun. Came to the edge of the woods and saw a farm wagon moving along, direction of Long Bridge Road. Piled high with last fall's hay. Crawled in in back for a breather and to put distance between him and the Yanks, without leaving trail.

After the better part of a slow hour, the road ran through woods again, so Davin dropped down from the hay and crawled in under the bushes to think it out. He could still hear the heavy artillery firing to the far north of him. He had no clear idea of what time it was, but he was dead solid in his mind now that it must be Stonewall Jackson up there. It must be, from the sharp and ugly character of the fight, and all that Watts had said.

He climbed a tree after a while and listened out the firing carefully. Sure'n hell it was somewhere up around Mechanicsville. He figured from the map, if, like Watts said, McClellan began to roll up like a rug under Jackson's pressure and get forced down across the Chickahominy toward the James, that it'd be on a route down, something like Mechanicsville—Gaines'

Mill—Cold Harbor—Savage Station—Frayser's Farm—Malvern Hill, because that's the way the roads lay. Having decided that, he went to sleep for the rest of daylight, because if McClellan was coming down that way, that would be the way for Davin to get north to join his own outfit. And night would be the best time to work his way through a hundred and five thousand Yankees.

That night he worked north as far as a place on his map called Tate & Riddell. Quite a road net joined there—Charles City Road, Long Bridge, Quaker Road—with connecting short roads across. Holed up to sleep the day off in a clump of rhododendrons, he couldn't sleep much because of Yankee troop movements all day. Passed the time by putting all of it on his map—infantry, cavalry, artillery—just as he'd been told to do in the balloon. But close to, this way, he could get the regimental numbers from the flags and what states they were from and approximately what time they passed, with arrows in which direction they were moving. It built up to quite a thing after a while, that maybe some general could use right handily.

The firing kept moving east for the three days Davin worked slowly toward it; until the twenty-eighth it was up north of Savage Station on the Richmond and York River Rail Road. Davin was getting a right decent span of mileage, considering he had to move slowly to avoid countersigns at night. But then, so was General Jackson getting good mileage, in spite of the fact he had to fight a hundred thousand Feds for it. Whatever, Stonewall Jackson and Davin were right close to joining up now, and as Davin holed up at sunup in a clump of maple on the Seven Mile Road, the whole character of the Yankee rear movement began to change. First, there were wounded wagonloads pulling out south. So many of them you could hardly keep count. A three-day slug-fight crop. Mechanicsville, Gaines' Mill, Old Cold Harbor wounded. Then there were regiments marching back. Badly mauled regiments, with batteries down to three guns, two, and sometimes only one. Horse cavalry with half the men afoot and straggling. Then heavy supply wagons. Ammunition, flour barrels, pork and tentage. Engineers with bridge equipment. Everything. And lying roadside in the brush, Davin got all of it on his map.

The Seven Days' Battle caught Davin as it swept past Watkins Mill, late the afternoon of the twenty-ninth, headed south for Frayser's Farm and Malvern Hill. Taliaferro's third brigade hot on the tail of McClellan pulling out of Savage Station. When you're close, you have to lie close on account of passwords and itchy trigger fingers. Davin waited until he saw the 23rd Virginia colors pass him in the skirmish line across the fields, then he got up and walked in toward the colors of the 10th Virginians moving down the road in reserve.

"Fella says he's out of Ashby's Cav'ry. Talks crazy. Says he came part way by b'loon and his pass run out. Better send him to the provost marshal…. Get along, bud; we got work coming up."

The provost said, "Got a map on him, hunh? Balloon? He's daffy! Must be a spy. There's General Jackson's topographical engineer over theah. Take him over to Captain Hotchkiss—mebbe's a major now. Let Hotchkiss decide, I'm busy."

The letdown after three days of working back through the enemy lines had Davin shaky inside by that time. He just stumbled along in a tired daze, like a man who's got his courage up to have the blacksmith pull his tooth—and the tooth's come clean without snagging off the roots. He handed over the map whenever they asked and just stood blinking from lack of sleep, and waiting, with Cousin Tandy's wedding dress still roped to his shoulder.

Young Hotchkiss frowned at him. "Look here," he said; "this is the whole axis of General Jackson's attack marked out, and General Jackson don't even tell his staff! And look here—here's almost the whole of McClellan's army movement behind the lines for the past three days, horse, men and guns. They are pulling out for the James to hold the high ground at Malvern Hill, you ask me! Keep that man close. If he tries to escape, shoot him!"

"I ain't agoin' nowhere," Davin said. "I just come."

Then suddenly across the road, there was Gin'ral Jackson himself, standing by his great horse with his officers grouped around him. White with dust and caked wet in the armpits with sweat through the jacket. His great round beard was scraggled from tugging at it three battle days. His face looked drawn to the bones under it, tight like a pudding cloth, from lack of sleep, but his back was as straight as a ramrod. He took the map from young Hotchkiss and glanced at it. Then for a moment he studied it intently, fingering out the road nets on it with the hand hit at Manassas—that always throbbed him after. Measuring mileage by laying the first two joints of the index finger to the road, then to the scale. Then, very slowly, he let the map hang to arm's length and he turned and looked south toward the battle thunder rolling down toward Frayser's Farm now, and he put his thumb and finger to his old Institute kepi visor where it was burred, and he pulled the hat tight, so's just not to hide the awful blue battle light of his eyes. Then he smiled ....

Davin didn't find Roan or his own outfit until after the Malvern Hill battle on July first, which left McClellan in full retreat to under his gunboats' covering fire on the James River. Didn't find him until after he'd got into Richmond again, during the lull.

In Richmond at the Summerhayes house on Broad Street behind the Governor's Mansion, Davin gave the dress to his Cousin Tandy.

"Oh, Davin, we've been expecting you!" she said. "Aunt Honor's got a three-year-old hidden out in our stable here for you. Eclipse blood." When Davin gave her the dress she said, "How perfectly sweet of you! You're a dear boy, but I can't possibly wear it!"

"Why not, Tandy? Don't it fit?"

"But it's not that at all! You just don't know Richmond girls, Davin. They just live and breathe this awful war in every fiber!"

"That so?"

"Of course it's so. How could we live if we weren't patriotic to the last drop of our blood! You see, they collected every silk dress in the Confederacy to make a balloon, and it got captured!"

"Oh, it did?"

"And no Richmond girl would ever think of wearing a silk——"

When he found Roan, Roan squinted at him hard. "Well, Dav," he said, "Gin'ral Jackson sure knew where to find you. He sure came and got you!"

"I didn't git to talk to him m'self," Davin said earnestly, "but is there going to be trouble about the pass running out? Can you fix it for me? You know I wouldn't——"

Roan considered it for a moment. "They were all for putting you through the sausage grinder for a spy. Until they put it to Gin'ral Jackson himself."

"Bad trouble?"

"Well," Roan drawled, "it's beyond anything I can do about the pass, if that's what you mean. With them all up in arms about how you got that map and what to do with you, Old Stonewall Jackson made the decision himself."

"What'd he say? Come on! Tell me!"

"Well," Roan said, "Stonewall just sort of smiled at them in that way he has, and handed them back the pass. Then he got on his horse, with your map in hand and 'Gentlemen,' he said, 'extend the man's pass!' "

So we have told a tale of half a war, and seen a nation half-born in the blood and anguish of its own labor pains. There is Second Manassas still to come—and Chancellorsville. The dreadful Wilderness and Gettysburg where the struggle attains immortal crescendo. There is the strangulation of the blockade which bled the dying Confederacy white; and the Mississippi actions, north and south, that double-knotted the ligature. Jackson dies and J. E. B. Stuart dies and the last of the glory dies with them. There is little but cussedness left—and pride of corps which can transcend all personal misery, and does. The will to go on against all odds, which is the rebirth of manhood, whenever it happens in history. Two lifetimes after Washington's ragged Continentals evacuated New York, the Army of Northern Virginia was forced to uncover Richmond.

> "On the way to Appomattox, the ghost of an army
> Staggers a muddy road for a week or so
> Through fights and weather, dwindling away each day."

Who today can see Appomattox as it was? Too much national dishonor follows on the echo of Booth's pistol shot. Degradation comes upon the land and men's hearts are twisted in black anger that was never there in combat.

At Appomattox there is the dignity of God, the quietude of honored death, for at Appomattox the Army of Northern Virginia is dead—but still upon its feet. *Dead in the presence of over-whelming Union force that has it penned so that one further step, one more shot is only madness. And madness is no longer in this thing. But discourtesy is and crassness is*—in the actions of *the goldenhaired Custer, for West Point could never make him a gentleman, nor a soldier. Nor could the dead Seventh Cavalry at the Big Horn.*

Two decent men however, meet in a quiet room and the war is ended.

All the way back to the Short Mountain country, Roan Catlett, Forney Manigault, and Davin Ancrum plodded in shock. Talk had left them gradually during the last four years so that there would have been little for them to have said even had victory kissed their shields. Roan was twenty-two with six wounds upon his body. Forney was just turned man to vote but his elbow would never bend again. Davin was just twenty, but a man so old in mind that his children would only find youth still in him when he dug down consciously to bring it up for them.

There was no heartbreak in that shock, no bitter stain of frustration. Certainly no guilt, for they had been fighting for their Country, not against it. The shock was impersonal and it beggared analysis. A gray shroud like the first reaction to a crippling blow, an apartness that stole the taste from food, the sunshine from the morning, the wine from the high, good air of the mountains. They walked three days in the little death of it, leading their gaunt horses until the strength built up in the animals once more.

Then strangely they were on their old boyhood road, three ghosts haunting it, coming to the first turning. When they reached it, Davin stopped. "Well, Gentlemen—" he said and he took off his abominable hat, holding it in his left hand. He held his right out to his cousin Forney. "Take care of yourself, Forney." To Roan, he said nothing beyond the grip of his fingers on Roan's. The tears flooded his eyes then and lifted his chin higher. They channeled the deep war grime of his face. He could not sob, for the muscles of his throat and chest were caught tight as fear had never caught them. Nor did he wipe the tears, for they were like slow blood from his soul that would not stop.

When he dropped Roan's hand, he shook his head once, short and sharp. Then he turned up his road—to farming, to storekeeping, to this and that that required no great mental effort, for his memory was always too strong upon his youth to allow anything else to encroach too heavily upon his mind—ever. At San Juan Hill long afterwards, as a fifty-three-year-old Major of Volunteers when the order came to advance on the Spanish blockhouse, Davin turned to his men and shouted "Come on, Boys—we'll drive the damyankees off that hill!"

At Forney's turnoff, they stopped again. Forney said, "Roan—I want you to think about it. I'll have to go to the University, my Dad's so set on it. Maybe at Charlottesville the thinking'll come straight for us again. At least it can't hurt us, doing nothing on good bourbon."

Roan shook his head. "Not me, Forney. I've got to work. It's the only way I can saddle the hate—not of anything particularly—but of all of it. Hate is like a man you have to wrestle hard. You can't let up until you break him...."

And much later that night at the Catlett place Roan said the same thing to his father.

"What work, Roan?"

"Body work, Sir. Sweating work. Muscle work that tires you gray to sleep."

"Where?"

"Texas way, Sir. There are a lot going. Land is cheap and the place is wide. It's not like I was your only son, Sir. You've got three to stay who haven't the reason I have for going. I fought for this land—and I lost it. I can't bear to see it any more!"

"Once before, Roan, you wanted to leave. Maybe leaving is in your soul. Maybe that's really why you went to war—to leave life itself."

Roan raised his head. "How do you mean?"

"Some men are always leaving. Job to job. Woman to woman. Ideas to ideas. But there's a funny thing about that—it catches up

when you grow old. Benedict Arnold asked his old Continental uniform coat be draped about him when he died. Deserters always have to turn in before the end to get their records straight. A man can live in far lands most of life but he hankers in his age to come back to where he was a boy—to where his people sleep. I didn't make that up. It's a law of life. Like the Ten Commandments. Nobody made them up. They are the sum total of man's moral experience throughout the ages. Where'd you get that golden mare, Roan? She's got Timoleon blood or I don't know horseflesh."

Roan started slightly as if he had heard something faintly down the midnight road. "I got her … after she shot Jason."

"Who shot Jason?"

"A little girl in Winchester—when I had to leave. Look here, Sir. Let's turn in. I've got to start for Winchester tomorrow, to take Lady back."

There were four chimneys left of the Lentaigne house, clutched to the sky like fingers of a stiff hand, with the two charred cross gables of Sheridan's mitre arching them. But Molly was there as she always would be. Sixteen that spring, chatelaine of her father's land, her father's house and her father's people when so little remained of any of it that for a moment there were only tears in Roan—but inside him. Not in his gaunt eyes.

Her dark hair was parted cleanly in the middle and braided tightly along each side. Her nose turned up just a tiny shade at the tip. Her waist was girl slender m the young flesh of womanhood. For a moment when she saw him walking up the old drive leading Lady, she stood stark and unbelieving, for the heritage of defeat was on her too—and she had been born to losing everything.

Then she laughed deep in her throat. Not a laugh really but a gentle sound of exquisite joy.

"Roan!" she said. "I knew you'd come back!"

ABOUT JAMES WARNER BELLAH

J AMES WARNER BELLAH HAS dedicated his writing life to an examination of Americans and their past and present way of life. *The Valiant Virginians* is his latest offering—a study of the private soldier of the Confederacy, written without white-pillared tidewater houses or crinolines, without the flamboyance of Scarlett O'Hara and the eternal swagger of fictional bright sabres.

Born in New York City three months before the turn of the present century, Mr. Bellah came of the last gasp of an ancient Irish family which has since acquired several more gasps, as he puts it, in the persons of his three sons, who range from a twenty-two-year-old soldier in the 44th Infantry Division to Stephen Hopkins Bellah, aged one and a half. His people have been lawyers and judges and part-time soldiers here for two-and-a-half centuries. A namesake, Captain James Bellah, fought as an infantry officer at Princeton, Brandywine, and Cooch's Bridge. John Bellah, for whom Mr. Bellah's middle son was named, was a soldier in the second war with Britain and explored well beyond the western waters of the Ohio country before 1809. A great-uncle was a Confederate naval officer. His own grandfather was Captain Charles Jefferson Johnson, 15th United States Infantry, who was wounded seven times from Harrison's Landing on— and who arrived at Appomattox in an ambulance, still in command of his company. His father raised a company of volunteers in the Spanish-American War.

The history of the United States was thus, in a way, a personal family record during Mr. Bellah's boyhood—of which record he says one thing pertinent: "Whether they came yesterday or three centuries ago, all Americans have one thing in common. They had and have the primeval courage to turn their backs forever on tradition and the scenes and habits of their childhood—to seek the elusive promise that lies in new lands. There was no going back nor is there today—and therein lies final dedication!"

Mr. Bellah was educated at Columbia College in New York City. His M. A. is in history (Georgetown University). He was privileged to sit as an undergraduate under the late John Erskine and had his first book published by Knopf, shortly after he took his A. B. His early story "Fear" in *The Saturday Evening Post* is still considered to be the finest story of flying ever written. His stories have gone into thirty-odd anthologies and been translated into fifteen languages. Books of his, by official request, are on the shelves of the Library of the Imperial War Museum in London and of the Bibliothèque de la Musée de la Guerre in Paris. The worksheets and original manuscripts of *The Valiant Virginians* were requested by Columbia University to become part of the permanent exhibit. The United States Military Academy at West Point has requested the original situation maps that Kenneth Fagg of *The Saturday Evening Post* art staff made for these stories, from air mosaics he supervised. Mr. Bellah has been informed that the Virginia Military Institute intends to confer an honorary degree upon him for his contribution to living Virginia history.

In setting the full perspective for his work, Mr. Bellah has lived and traveled and written the world over. China in the days of Chang Tso Teng—and later in the days of General Stilwell. The Federated Malay States, Burma, India, and Arabia, Europe from the time of many kings to the time of many upstart threats and unconscionable political turmoil. Mexico, South and Central America (he was a member of the crew of the first plane to fly mail from Miami to Panama), New Guinea, Australia, and

Japan. Travels lightly told of in his tongue-in-cheek autobiography, *Irregular Gentleman.*

He has been a soldier. In France at seventeen in the first World War, he went shortly into the Royal Flying Corps from the Transport Service and ended the war as a de Haviland pilot with the 117th Squadron R.A.F. Briefly thereafter he was a captain in General Haller's expedition for the relief of Poland. In World War II he started as a platoon commander, 16th Infantry, First Infantry Division. He served thereafter, in one capacity or another, in every staff echelon from battalion to theatre. In Southeast Asia he was on Viscount Mountbatten's staff. He served with General Stilwell at Taihpa Ga and Mainkwang, along the Tanai River. He was attached temporarily, through the death in action of his British opposite number, to General Orde Charles Wingate's Chindits. He flew in the point glider with Phil Cochran's tiny airborne task force that seized and held the target "Broadway" deep in central Burma, from which airhead the 3rd Indian Division operated to cut the supply lines of the four Japanese divisions that then threatened Imphal.

His novel of that war was *Ward Twenty,* a work seldom equalled for its stark acceptance of the cost of war.

At present Mr. Bellah lives in Santa Monica where the Pacific washes his doorstep. Eleven years ago he married Helen Lasater Hopkins, daughter of the late Colonel N. Hopkins, U.S.A., of the Marshal Mission. Mrs. Bellah does most of his detailed research once he blocks it out—in the intervals between the continuing task of raising young sons that the progression may go on.

Of *The Valiant Virginians* Mr. Bellah says: "Few men know how a story is born, or a group of characters. I lay in hospital two years ago thinking of the more pleasant places I had been in my living and suddenly the Shenandoah Valley was the most pleasant of them all. But it has always lived fullest for me when the ghosts of Jackson's men march through it. I can, in my profession, destroy time and space at will. I destroyed the hospital and went back to live in the '60's where the greatest peril was a minie ball and the greatest joy the smile of a soft-eyed girl in Winchester. So was born *The Valiant Virginians* and if you do not believe they live, I swear to you that they do still, for at sundown of a Sunday not a month gone—from the pleasant back verandah of Charles and Mildred Pickett's at Fairfax—we saw three of Stuart's troopers lead their mounts in for water. Catlett, Ancrum, and Manigault.

"It was so unusual a sight in 1953 on a hot Virginia evening, that the portraits, too, reached for a glass as the great silver tray passed once more!"

FLETCHER PRATT was born in Buffalo, New York, in 1897 and has written a number of books on military subjects, including Ordeal by Fire, *a famous and highly esteemed one-volume history of the Civil War.*

Printed in Great Britain
by Amazon

79735286R00089